AF271444

THE EVOLUTION OF NORA O'BRIEN PACHECO

KEVIN O'FLAHERTY

KEVIN O'FLAHERTY

Theses stories are based on real places using imaginary characters.

Like the internet, Artificial Intelligence will play a bigger role in our
daily life. With regards to literature, I see it as a tool, but I haven't used
it yet.

ISBN:978-84-09-61465-3

E-mail: Sapereaudelibris@gmail.com

 Created with Vellum

For Tommy

Quo Vadis?

There are many roads to travel.

What will you do if you choose the wrong path?

Will you sit still and give up?

Or will you get up to overcome your challenges?

If you get lost, remember a lesson that I have eventually learned.

The universal values are more important than ever.

Let them guide you to overcome your fear.

There is only one constant in life:

I love you forever.

Which way will you go?

AMATOR LIBRORUM

Anno Domini:

Ex libris:

Ex dono:

PART I

Bilbao, Spain. Nora stopped at her front door to dry the tears. She waved her hand in front of her face to cool her red, puffy eyes and took a deep breath before walking into the kitchen. It was small and clean with walls generously decorated with inexpensive artwork bought from local artists or found in second-hand shops.

Her mother jerked her head backwards at Nora's appearance. 'What's the matter, honey? You look defeated. Are they still picking on you at school?'

Nora frowned and hung her head lower. 'Yeah, there are a few classmates who bother me.'

Her mother sighed. 'You get along well with most of your classmates and your teachers like you. Why do you let the opinions of classmates that you don't like bother you so much? Their opinions should not matter. We all go through difficult times, even though you think it's only you who is having a stressful situation. Most of the time, they bully because they are immature. If what they say bothers you, they'll keep it up.'

She put her hand on Nora's shoulder. 'Some of them may be jealous of you, because you get high marks and have good friends.* Others are not happy with themselves, or have a terrible home life, so it makes them feel good to see others in pain. As you know, emotionally hurt people like to see others hurt.'

Her mother reached out and pulled her into a hug. 'Don't worry! School is ending soon, and the summer holiday will start. Do you remember the holiday in Wales last year? We explored all the castles and discovered that boarding school by chance. The three of us took a tour and found out the school was built on old church grounds. We talked about you studying there for the summer to improve your English and become more independent. When we got back home, we filled out the online application. Well, you have been accepted!' Wrinkles appeared in deep furrows around her eyes and mouth as she grinned.

Seventeen-year-old Nora's eyes widened, and her body stiffened at the news. She was almost as tall as her mother when she stood straight. Side by side, there was no doubting their relationship. They both had the same large brown eyes and the same brown hair, which was separated only by the style and the streaks of grey that ran through her mother's chignon bun. Nora ran her fingers through her shoulder-length hair, letting it fall back into its regular middle parting.

'When are we going?'

---

* High marks are good grades in American English

Her mother put her arm on her shoulder. 'You are going by yourself. Your father and I plan to make some adjustments to the house in the coming months. The school staff will watch over everything.'

Her mother turned off the oven and looked at Nora.

'As I said, your father and I thought about something different this summer.'

Her father was older than her mother and his hair was losing its brown hue. With age, it had taken on a new personality and now never looked combed, always pointing upwards in spikes of grey and white.

'He wanted to tell you too, but he went to an appointment. The boarding school offers a two-month course. You and your father loved to explore and look at the architecture of the place. He thinks of himself as a world adventurer, but he is just an old chubby dreamer!' she said with laughter. 'Anyway, you'll find the school absolutely brilliant.'

Her mother's confidence and warm smile made Nora feel better. She loved the chance to practise English and explore different places and often drew sketches of the buildings in her notebook with her parents. She went to her bedroom to think about what she would take, but alone in her room her stomach churned. Nora tried to push away her anxiety by turning her attention to what she should pack. She pulled a medium size suitcase and a backpack out from under her bed and opened them up ready to pack in her treasured belongings and a few outfits to wear. Clothes were not too important to her, so as her parents often did while travelling, she wanted to pack lightly. Looking around her small, tidy room deciding what to pack, her eyes were drawn to the many historical oil paintings arranged with precision on the walls and the large world map above her desk. The map was dotted with tiny flags showing the places she had visited or wanted to visit. On her desk, there was her bug and rock collection, a retro digital camera and a travel journal packed with architectural drawings and sketches on each of the pages. She picked up the journal and flicked through the pages, a smile crossing her lips. She loved her few belongings.

A short while later, Nora went to meet her best friend Ainhoa to tell her the good news. They hugged as they met.

'Do you remember I told you about the boarding school in Wales last year?' Nora spoke quickly, the excitement in her voice impossible to ignore. 'My parents applied for me to study there this summer. Well, the school has accepted me!'

'Wow! That's so exciting,' Ainhoa said, while she adjusted her thick, black-rimmed glasses. 'I wish I could go too.'

Ainhoa put on her trainers and wiggled her feet, admiring the three-inch platform soles of her new shoes. Her dog, noticing the movement, banged its tail on the floor before stretching and making its way to sit by the door in readiness for its walk. Ainhoa ignored the dog's growing impatience and stepped forward to straighten the frame of her large bug collection displayed on the wall.

'We're going to visit our family for a few weeks in the summer.' She looked disappointed as they walked out of the house. 'It's nice, but not exciting. Olatz is also going on holiday, so I'll be here on my own. What am I going to do without you two?'

'Ainhoa, you'll be ok. I'll write and send photos to you.'

～

A month later. Wales, the United Kingdom. The Cambrian School was built in typical English architecture style, with buildings made of red brick or square blocks. The spacious grounds held a museum, a church and a large sports pitch. The rest of the area was left to open grass fields. An old stone wall, almost two metres high, encircled the campus and separated it from the surrounding dense woodland and the bubbling waters of the River Towy.

History has it that the native Britons inhabited the area. Then the Romans conquered the region and built their villas and left an imprint of their customs and language. After they left, monks built on the old Briton settlement. Like any successful group, the well-organised monks were hard-working and persistent and made the area prosperous. Centuries later, the kings of England, looking for wealth and land, took control of the property. Time marched on and they eventually sold the land to private owners who made it into a school.

The school's main office was sparsely furnished with only a simple pedestal desk resting on a polished wooden floor. Above the desk, a large white and green Welsh flag, with a red dragon in its centre hung on the wall, glaring out at all the visitors who entered the room.

Llewellyn, a teacher, walked into the director's office.

Despite its thickness, the beard didn't hide his youthfulness. 'Have you finished choosing the final student candidates for the summer?'

The school director, Gwynfor, had a look of great pressure on his face. 'Yes,' he said, 'I have their class assignments ready. More than half of the candidates will get some type of scholarship to lower the cost.'

Llewellyn shrugged. 'Why do you always have a weak spot for students who cannot pay their full tuition fees?'

Gwynfor put down the paperwork he'd been clutching and stood up. 'Because they deserve it. They are bright and inquisitive but lack financial means to study.'

'You know we will be better off financially by only allowing the ones who can pay full tuition. We have spent a lot of money on the museum's renovations.'

'I am well aware of our finances,' Gwynfor grunted in frustration. 'Many students who pay full room and board deserve to study here. Their families understand the value of education and are willing and able to pay for it, but others still deserve the chance. The ones without the means to pay for it. Those who have been in stressful situations in their country or even suffered bullying. We know that given the chance they too can excel academically. We have seen the effects unstable countries or bullying can have on a student and now we are the administrators and teachers at this school, we have a duty to allow more diverse students in.'

Llewellyn persisted. 'Yes, that is good of you, but it puts pressure on the school's finances. We are going to have to raise tuition fees and accept more students who can pay full room and board soon.'

'I have already sent the notices to the students´

houses that we have accepted them.' He returned to his chair. 'By the way, we have the replicas of paintings arriving at the museum this week. I'll need a hand receiving the shipment. Although they are replicas, they are expensive, because of the artist who painted them. The other teachers agree that having replicas of well-known art in our art classes is helpful. Also, the ongoing construction of the two new sections of the museum, during the summer months, makes it more complicated.'

On the first day of school, Gwynfor and the other teachers waited in Cymru Hall, the principal building on campus, to welcome the students. A teacher stood at the head of the auditorium, facing everybody.

'Good morning, students. I am Seren. Welcome to the Cambrian School and Wales!'

Everyone's eyes focussed on Seren. Despite her advancing age, signs of beauty were still very clear. Her skin was olive and distinct facial features that set her apart from others were framed by her long wavy dark hair. Seren was atypical for a Welsh woman, but she wore a daffodil pin on her jacket and spoke with a strong Welsh accent as her commanding voice rang through the room.* Her direct approach and command of her audience made Nora have no doubt that Seren was highly competent and could handle a crowd of teenagers in an orderly fashion without being too nice or nervous.

---

* Daffodil is the national flower of Wales

She explained to the students, 'We are going to put you in your groups for classes and also assign your roommates.'

At the initial gathering of the groups, Nora met her two roommates, Gwendolyn and Elsi. Nora liked Gwendolyn instantly. She was open and straightforward, with a friendly smile and a curious spirit. She had fair skin, hair and eyes.

'Everybody calls me Gwen,' Nora's new roommate said. 'My family is from a mining town. My grandparents were miners. I speak Welsh with my father, but my mum mostly speaks English. We say bore da for good morning, diolch for thanks, hwly fawr to say goodbye.' She looked at Nora. 'How do you say a few words in Basque?'

Nora held her head high. 'We say kaixo to say hello, agur to say goodbye and eskerrik asko for thank you.'

'Wow!' said Gwen, 'my language teacher told us that Basque is the oldest language in Europe and Welsh is the oldest language in the United Kingdom. What about you, Elsi? What language is spoken in Peru?'

Elsi's dark black hair shined in the light. 'I'm from Lima and most people speak Spanish, but we also speak Quechua, the language the Incas spoke. My elderly neighbour speaks it. In Quechua, kawsaypac means to live, munay to love and allianchu for hello.'

Gwen smiled. 'So, we have something in common with ancient languages.'

There were three enormous suitcases next to Gwen's bed, and Nora pointed at them. 'Who brought all this luggage for two months?'

'Well, I did,' Gwen said, looking down. 'I prepared for any emergency.'

She asked Nora and Elsi with a look of doubt, 'You brought a small suitcase and a backpack?'

Elsi pointed to her two small bags as well and they all laughed together.

～

On the first day of class, the teacher Seren greeted them. 'Ok, quiet down, class,' she said, her voice calm and confident. 'This is Art History. The goals are researching works of art and writing papers, but the overall goal is discovery. Discovery of yourselves. You need to develop a strong sense of finding your place in the world. What do you believe in? How will you overcome challenges in life? Will you stand up for something that you believe is right or stay quiet and later regret it?'

She walked in front of the class, looking directly at each and every student as she spoke. 'Along the way, you'll face obstacles. They come in all shapes and sizes. They can come from the always-changing technology and the lack of knowledge to adapt to it. More often, obstacles come from the people that you meet. I believe working with people is the key to getting goals accomplished. I also believe working with people could be very frustrating as you accomplish those goals. When you do something that they don't like, they usually insult you behind your back. If you report it, they deflect blame and tell another version.'

She stopped walking around the room and paused, her head down as if in thought. She raised her head to look directly at the students. 'We are going to do group projects. Sometimes you will find working in groups stressful, so you'll need to work it out between yourselves to finish the assignments. The first project is this...' She began writing something on the chalkboard. 'I want you to learn the history of the school and write an essay. You can look up information on a computer, but I prefer going to the library and checking out well-written books on the subject. There are a few good books, especially an old leather book that was written by the founder of the school. We will review the assignment in more detail on Monday.'

After class, Nora had a question to ask Seren about the topic. Seren smiled at her and asked, 'What's an Irish girl doing coming here to study for the summer?'

'I am not Irish. I am from Bilbao, the Basque country, in Spain.'

'Ahhh,' said Seren. 'I do hear a slight accent. You speak English well. Is your father Irish?'

'No. He's American, but his parents were from Ireland. He speaks English to me, but I usually speak Spanish at home with my mum and Spanish or Basque with my friends. I learn the Basque language at school, so I rarely speak academic English. My parents thought I should practise more. We often go on holidays abroad and we like architecture, history and photography. That's how we found Cambrian last year.'

Nora and most of her classmates went to the next class. The teacher, Llewellyn, was also comfortable and direct. As the students walked into his applied mathematics classroom, they noticed a lever and fulcrum, a pulley, wheel and screw on his table.

'We are going to solve maths equations using practical hands-on methods,' he said. 'I want you to bring maths to life so that you can better understand it. You know that machines help us work in a faster and easier way. We usually see machines as beyond our comprehension, but they are made up of simple parts. Most people just want to finish the job and move on.'

He walked closer to the table where the tools were and continued talking. 'Look at this lever and fulcrum. It's used for lifting heavy loads. The mathematician Archimedes once said that if he had a long enough lever, he could lift the world.'*

He put down the tools and walked to the middle of the class. 'We will have an exam next month. It is practical hands-on work using these tools to figure out equation problems.'

Nora liked the way he taught. It was obvious he had experience and was enthusiastic about his subject. In contrast to new teachers, who tried being too nice to the students so that everybody liked them, he was direct and firm and controlled his class, so they were never too loud or disrespectful.

After classes were finished, Seren met Llewellyn in the staff room. She was keen to discuss her first observations about the new students. 'We sometimes get letters of recommendation from teachers about a particular student telling us why they think their student deserves a chance to study here.' Seren walked to the window as she was speaking. 'We got five letters from Nora's teachers who think very highly of her.' She paused and pointed to the field. 'Look outside. What do you see?'

Llewellyn crossed to the window. The primary group

---

* Greek inventor from the ancient city of Syracuse, Sicily.

of students were in a big circle and there at the edge of the group Nora stood with her friend looking at the different trees.

He wasn't interested and changed the topic. 'Have you heard about the museum remodelling? I would rather get a pay rise than refurbish an old building.' He tugged at a thread on the cuff of his jacket as if to emphasise his point. Seren ignored the action.

'I don't mind,' Seren said. 'The paintings and sculpture classes help them understand art better.'

'That's fine coming from an art teacher. However, a bigger pay cheque would do me better.'

Nora was with Gwen, walking around the campus. 'I want to go to the library to check out the old book that Seren told us about,' Nora said.

Gwen nodded. 'Let's get Elsi first, then go to the library. I can see the other students are returning to their dormitory.'

As the three girls entered the library, they saw a boy named Owain from their class. He smiled at them as he walked past them towards the exit.

'I saw him going towards his building before,' Elsi said in a surprised tone. 'That is farther away than ours. How did he get there and back here so fast?'

They stopped and all three frowned when Gwen whispered, 'He's a troublemaker by the way he looks.'

They asked the librarian about the old leather book. She said one of their classmates had already checked it out.

'He got the leather book already,' Gwen gasped.

'Don't worry. There are others we can check out,' Nora assured her friends. With a look of disappointment, they headed further inside the library. The library was a wonderful place, with wooden bookshelves with loads of old books, large plants and historic oil paintings in each room. Nora loved the idea of researching by reading old books because that reminded her of her collection of books back home.

As the first few weeks passed, one evening after dinner, Nora went to meet Gwen and Elsi. Her two friends had already left and were talking to a group of girls outside the front entrance of their residence hall.

One girl said to Gwen and Elsi, 'Nora's notebook is full of architectural drawings and she talks about her prehistoric sharks' teeth and bug collections. It's so weird! How do you put up with her in your dorm room?'

As Nora approached, the girl whispered, 'Oh look, she's coming. Come on, let's not wait for her!'

Elsi and Gwen looked at the girl and then at each other. Neither looked friendly towards her.

'Hey, Jane,' Gwen said. 'Do me a favour and stop talking about Nora like that. She's our friend.'

Jane's face turned red. 'Oh, ok,' came her weak response. She turned and joined the other girls.

Nora walked up to them. 'Hey, what's up? Was that Jane?'

Gwen smiled and grabbed Nora's and Elsi's arm gently and said, 'Let's go for a walk and talk about

tomorrow. Have you tried our Welsh cakes or bara brith?*
I'll bring some tomorrow from the local bakery.' As they
walked, Gwen looked around before she spoke. 'Some
girls like Owain.'

'He stays mostly by himself,' Elsi added.

Nora listened to her friends and smiled.

It was getting late. They saw the director Gwynfor
walking fast towards the museum. Nora turned to her
friends. 'What do you think about the teachers?'

'I like them,' answered Elsi. They all seem to be
interested in teaching. Even the director is nice. They say
he was a student here.'

Gwen nodded in agreement.

While returning to their residence hall, there stood
Owain, the boy from the library, talking to an adult at the
corner of the building. He turned away from the adult
and walked towards the residence entrance. He was red-
faced. He walked past the girls, but this time, he didn't
greet them. He was carrying a backpack with a long
cylinder tube poking out from inside and hurried inside
the residence. Nora thought about her art classes and
using a similar tube to carry paintings.

'Wow!' said Gwen. 'Did you see him? His face was
bright red.'

Elsi looked at the man walking away. 'Was he talking
to a teacher?'

Nora shrugged. 'No, I don't think so, but it was too
dark to tell.'

'Come on,' commanded Gwen. 'It's getting late. Let's

---

* Welsh cakes, a sweet flat bread baked on a griddle. Bara brith is a
traditional bread flavoured with dried fruits.

go back in.' The three girls continued chatting as they walked back to their dormitory.

The following day, a group of students went to hang out in a small park close to town. In the centre of the park, there was a water fountain with a colourful flower bed surrounding it. Along the edges of the square, there were wooden benches for sitting. The three girls had brought juice and bara brith. They found an empty bench underneath a tree that would give them shade to escape the afternoon sun. Owain came with his two roommates to hang out with the girls.

On a bench close by, a man sat down wearing a wool jacket and a tattered hat. He took off his hat and placed it next to him, letting his long, unwashed hair fall to his shoulders. When a smell reached the students´ bench, they looked across at him and he stared back at them with a look of defiance, waiting for them to walk away, as he had seen happen many times before. He lay down and began muttering to himself. The students could not understand the incomprehensible words and smirked at each other. He couldn't have noticed them but even so, he sat up suddenly and turned to stare. He tilted his head as he did so, and a flutter of recognition passed his face as he looked at their uniforms. They quickly diverted their eyes to avoid his stare. One student whispered that the man was once a student at the school many years ago. The man continued to mumble, seemingly incoherently, as he lay back down, and they grinned, thinking it was funny.

Nora took a few remaining fruit juices and the rest of the bara brith bread and approached the homeless man.

She spoke to him in English. 'Hi.'

The man sat up and looked at her suspiciously.

'We have extra fruit punch and bara brith. Would you like them?' she asked hesitantly.

Her friends had stopped in surprise to watch her. The man's face slightly changed. His eyes relaxed and his face became less tense. A small smile crossed his lips, exposing missing teeth.

'Yes,' he said as he lifted his dirty hands to take them. He had had a long, hard night, and he tore at the bara brith in large bites. Nora smiled gently and handed him the juice before turning back towards her friends again.

A short while later, the three girls returned to campus, Gwen said, 'You know, that was a friendly gesture that you made to the homeless man.'

Nora nodded. 'Well, we had finished eating and we had leftovers, and he seemed to be hungry.'

'I know, but It's better to stay away from him.'

'Yeah, ok.'

Elsi looked down the hall and pointed. 'What's all that noise about?' The three looked down the hall. They saw Owain walking away from the group of boys and girls who had gathered at the entrance. He was wearing a backpack. The three girls approached the group of students, who were talking excitedly and fast.

One girl repeated what the group had said.

'Someone stole from the museum last night. They found a few paintings in the office of Director Gwynfor.' The girl continued speaking fast. 'He has not been charged because it could be anyone. He is on leave until further notice.'

Nora and her two friends looked at each other with a look of disbelief.

~

Later that evening, the three girls went to the library to study.

'It's so strange. It makes little sense,' Nora said, with a shrug of her shoulders. 'A person wouldn't steal something and then put it in their belongings, only to be discovered by the police. That's way too basic. Besides, even though he is not the friendliest, he seemed sincere about his work and love of art.'

'He wasn't the one who notified the police about the theft,' replied Gwen. 'The museum caretaker came in early and noticed it and notified campus security. Later on, the custodian found a stash of art in his office. Maybe he didn't have time to move it.'

Elsi gestured to her two friends, 'Hey look, there's Owain. It looks like he's working on a drawing.'

The friends continued to work at their study and an hour passed before any of them spoke again.

'Look,' Elsi pointed in Owain's direction, 'he is getting up.'

'He's probably going to get more books.' Nora returned to her own book, but after ten minutes, Owain hadn't returned back to his table.

Gwen looked left and right. 'What happened to him?'

Elsi pointed to a hall. 'I saw him go down this hallway, or maybe the one next to it.'

'Let's go find him and see what he's up to,' whispered Nora.

The three girls searched both hallways but didn't find him. They returned to their table and noticed he had left his books. They went to see what he was doing. 'Art books,' Nora gasped.

Gwen turned the pages of a book. 'Could he be the one involved with the theft? He is one of the few students whose parents studied here. He knows the school better than anyone.'

Elsi made a doubtful gesture. 'Why would he take the painting?'

'He looks like a troublemaker,' answered Nora. 'We have to follow him next time.'

Gwen looked at her phone. 'Come on, it's late, let's go back to the dorm.'

Later that evening, in the dorm, Nora called her parents by video chat. 'Hi, Mum! I miss you a lot. Where's Papi?'

Her mother adjusted the computer screen. 'You know him. He is busy running an errand.'

'Ok. I also called Ainhoa, but she hasn't called back yet.'

Her mother sighed. 'I don't know. I hope everything is fine. She's on summer holiday like you. Try again next week.'

She told her mother about her classes and said that she enjoyed studying English. Although, she admitted that speaking English with her father was a lot easier than reading and writing and using academic words that she had rarely used before.

One night, Nora was coming back from the library when Owain came out of nowhere twenty feet in front of her. He was alone as he walked into the entrance of the residence hall. He paused. His posture was watchful. It surprised her when he didn't go straight to the boys' dormitories, but instead went into a long, dark hall. *This is the chance to see what he is doing.*

She watched him through the window, half expecting him, or someone else, to see her peeking through it. She waited. He didn't return. It wasn't uncommon for a girl to be in the main entrance of the boys' section, but still, it was awkward. Nora entered and walked down the hall where she had seen him go. The hall wasn't too long, and it stopped at the wall that had a bookcase. There was one door used by the custodians, and a few windows.

Nora whispered under her breath, 'He must have gone down this hall. But where is he?'

She looked around and spun as she heard a noise coming from behind her. The old wooden bookcase opened, and a shadow appeared to be exiting. Nora let out a gasp, which was followed by a weak cry from her throat. It was Owain! He came from behind the bookcase and looked frightened. It also surprised him to see Nora standing there looking at him.

'What are you doing here?' He sounded nervous and unsure of what to do next.

'What are YOU doing here?' came her reply. They looked at each other for what seemed like an eternity until Nora broke the silence. 'Are there tunnels?'

Owain had found his composure and his previous insecurity had turned to defiance. He stayed silent.

She repeated the question. 'Come on, what are you up to? Have you been stealing things around the campus?'

She half expected him to avert his eyes, in a sign that he was lying. But he didn't look down. Instead, he looked right at her saying, 'I use the tunnels. My father mentioned them to me. He told me he used them with some friends when he studied here. No one knows about them.'

Nora again looked up and down the hall. It was empty and a light smattering of dust on the wooden floor showed it was barely used. The hidden door in the bookcase was hardly noticeable too except for a clear smear where the dust had been swept away.

Owain continued. 'These tunnels were for short cuts or in troubled times back in the day. The previous school director had locked or sealed up the passages. However, it looks like someone opened the locks to the tunnels recently. Besides,' he shrugged, 'if you knew about them, you would have used them too.'

Nora looked down because she knew he was right.

He narrowed his eyes. 'Why am I a thief? Yes, I checked out the book from the library using the tunnels. There are underground tunnels that connect many buildings. I like art. I have been in art and music classes since I was young. The canvas that I have been carrying is mine. I paint after classes. Did you think I took the paintings? It makes you feel good to think like that.'

She crossed her arms. 'You looked arrogant and suspicious.'

'Do you think I am arrogant? Why? Because I don't socialise with you. I explore on my own.'

'Who were you talking with that night? You looked upset.'

He responded with a heavy sigh, 'That was my father. He visited me for the afternoon.'

He remembered what his father had said:

His father had asked, 'Do you like school?'

Owain had replied with a downward look, 'It's ok.'

'How are your teachers and roommates?'

'They're ok.'

'You always find a few friends along the way,' his father said. 'Your mother and I wanted you to socialise more. You spend a lot of time alone. You are always observing the night sky, reading or drawing.'

His father put a hand on his son's shoulder and said, 'That's fine. We want you to meet more people. That's all.'

'I know, but I am comfortable in my room.'

'That's why we signed you up for the summer,' his father insisted. 'We want you to socialise more.'

Owain's face became twisted 'Ok, ok. It's only a few more weeks.'

'Good. It's getting late. You'd better go back in. We love you.'

Nora had a surprised expression on her face. 'Ahhh! I didn't know. Can you show me the tunnels? I would like to explore.'

Owain hesitated. 'I didn't want everybody to know about the tunnels, but I hear noises and I think it's better to explore them with somebody.' He nodded in agreement. 'Ok, I'll show you the way.'

'Not now.' She didn't want to explore the tunnel with a boy she didn't trust. 'I'll ask my friends to go with us.'

He shrugged his shoulders, 'Once you tell them, they will tell more students and we can get in trouble. It's better to keep quiet.'

'I trust them.'

'Ok, tomorrow. I have to finish my homework now.'

They left the hall. The light on the wall reflected a shadow of a person. Then the bookcase closed slowly.

Nora told Gwen and Elsi about the encounter with Owain.

'I want to explore the tunnels,' she said. 'Do you want to go with me?'

'Yeah,' answered Gwen with a big grin.

Nora looked at Elsi. 'What about you, Elsi? Do you want to come?'

'No, I don't want to get in trouble. I have to study anyway.'

'Ok. That's fine. I understand.'

The following night, Nora went to her dormitory to get Gwen. She opened the door and found a huge backpack and asked, 'What are you going to do with that?'

Gwen raised her arms. 'Just in case we get hungry, or thirsty or cold, we'll have enough to survive for a few days.'

'Leave it! We won't need it. We are not going on a safari!'

They met Owain at the entrance to the residence hall.

He greeted them and said, 'After the tunnels, I want to show you something.'

Nora looked at him suspiciously. 'What do you want to show us?'

'It's difficult to explain. It could get cold at night. Did you bring a jacket?'

Gwen smiled at Nora and said, 'I told you so.'

The tunnels were dark, damp and made of brick. Owain took out an old-fashioned torch and turned it on. Both Nora and Gwen blinked at the blackness, opening their eyes wider as they struggled to see. Their hearts were beating fast with excitement and their breathing was shallow. After a few minutes they reached a split in the tunnel. He turned left and the girls followed. With their eyes now accustomed to the darkness, they could recognise signs written in Latin showing the direction of the tunnels.

Nora looked at him. 'Your father told you about the tunnels?'

'Yeah, he told me he used to explore with Gwynfor and Llewellyn, who are now teachers, and that homeless person at the park the other day. I think his name is Markel. My dad said that Gwynfor and Llewellyn made a lot of trouble.'

Nora frowned and tilted her head. 'That homeless man's name is Markel?' She paused as she processed this information. 'Well, he must be from the Basque country.'

Gwen spoke up. 'How do you know?'

'He was speaking in Basque to himself at the park.'

Gwen turned to Owain. 'When was the last time you were in the tunnels?'

'Hmm, it was four days ago. I was in the tunnel to the

library, and I saw a light coming from the tunnel to the church.'

Nora gasped. 'Four days ago. That was the night of the theft. Why did you run out of the tunnel last night?'

'I was going to explore,' he said with an exasperated sigh, 'but I heard some noise from a tunnel. I got scared and turned back to the bookcase entrance. That's how I ran into you last night.'

Gwen grunted. 'Did you see who it was?'

'No. I don't think I'll be going down by myself again for some time either,' he said, shifting the torch to his other hand. 'It is easy to talk about exploring the tunnels, but it's dark and your mind plays tricks on you.'

He took them to the Gothic church. It was inspiring to see during the day with its large stained-glass windows and stone gargoyles above the entrance. At night, in the tunnel, it felt more sinister. The church became more secular and was for social events for the diverse student population. The interior still had a church-like layout with statues of saints in niches on the wall and brown wooden benches on either side of the aisles. There was a long middle aisle leading up to the altar, with adjacent hallways on either side of it.

Nora liked the architecture and stained-glass windows. She thought every old building had a story to tell. Very few students even bothered to look at the architecture. She often sketched the buildings of the school in her travel notebook, writing notes and comments about the history of each building to remember her travels.

They arrived at the hidden door that led to one of the side halls. Owain slowly pushed open the heavy wooden door. It creaked as he did so. Together they walked into a dark hall that had old furniture and damaged statues of saints. The entrance of the hall had a large iron gate that was open. They headed toward the centre aisle and faced the altar. On the altar was a large wooden pulpit, sitting high above to the right. Behind the pulpit sat the control panel that operated the music, church bells and lights. They turned around to look at the entrance of the church opposite the altar. Above the entrance doors, on the back wall, was a large stained-glass window designed to look like a flower opening up its petals in response to the light that streamed in. The vibrant colours were spectacular as the moonlight streaming through began to dance on the stone floor.

Owain commented, 'It faces the east.'

'So what?' Gwen said, not understanding the significance.

'The sun rises in the east. It's a fantastic sight to see with the sun rising and the light reaching the altar. It's symbolic.'

Nora walked to the opposite hall of the one they had entered from the tunnel. This hall, too, had a large iron gate at the entrance, and as they entered, she noticed the walls covered with paintings. There was something curious about the paintings, and she was just about to mention it to her friends when Owain signalled them to leave.

The building that housed the artworks was a warehouse, but now it's a museum and art studio. It was an oval building that had four hallways branching out from the main aisle. From above it looked like a turtle lying flat. In the studio, the students had their art classes and the museum itself held mostly oil paintings, large ceramic Greek bowls and objects from around the world.

Nora took the torch from Owain as they arrived at a side hall. She wanted to walk down the main gallery. Gwen joined her and together they walked past walls filled with large replica paintings from famous artists. The light of the old torch nudged back the darkness. Only Owain had walked this path before, and the girls found it both thrilling and frightening at the same time – alone in the building, exploring at night, without a thought about the consequences.

There were other tunnels that they didn't explore. Some were sealed. Others, the much darker ones, they avoided. After exploring, he took Nora and Gwen to the old Celtic path that led to the wall that surrounded the school grounds. They had to climb the wall next to a maple tree and a large half-buried rock. They jumped down to an open field near the ruins of a Roman villa – it was a popular site for students and tourists, alike, to visit. The River Towy ran alongside the campus, passing under a stone bridge that led to the town of Carmarthen. Nora and Gwen looked at each other with hesitant glances.

Owain pointed toward the sky. 'Look up!'

Both girls looked up and saw the night sky sparkling with dots of light as far as the eye could see. He took out a portable telescope from his backpack and passed it to Nora.

'Very few appreciate the night-time sky. I already asked some of my flatmates to come and see it, but they weren't interested. You can see a few constellations with your eye, but with the telescope, you can see a lot better.'

Nora brought the telescope to her eye and adjusted the focus. Instantly she saw the details in the moon and the brightness of the stars. She exhaled as she handed the telescope to Gwen.

Gwen was equally as enthralled by the sight. 'I have seen photos of galaxies and nebulas in bloom. It's beautiful.'

Owain looked at her. 'That's a romantic version of space. It's actually cold, dark and violent. Humans are explorers. I think astronauts will build habitats on the moon within the next ten years. Everybody thinks there are alien life forms because of all the films and documentaries, but I read an interesting book that states we could be alone in the universe. The conditions to create life are extremely rare, and even if there is intelligent life, they are in the same dilemma as we are.'

Nora frowned. 'What dilemma?'

'The universe is so vast; it would take hundreds of years to reach the next galaxy. We don't have the technology to travel at the speed of light or carry food and supplies. Without the ozone layer, there is harmful radiation, and zero gravity deteriorates our bodies. Alien life forms, if they exist, face the same laws of physics. Our scientists here, who work for space agencies, have more degrees from top universities on their walls and dream about space travel, while their own world is on fire. Even to reach planets in our solar system would take a few years, and the best planet is Mars, with no oxygen or life form other than possible water. Astronauts can use water as fuel to go to other planets further than Mars. Water is made up of hydrogen and oxygen. They can make hydrogen gas for fuel, but it's useless for long voyages.'*

Gwen put down the telescope. 'You know a lot about astronomy.'

'I was hanging out in my bedroom bored one summer morning. My father asked me if I wanted to camp at Eryri (Eh-ru-re) National Park near Yr Wyddfa Mountain (Er with-va). † I said no. They packed and were leaving. I looked around my room with nothing to do and decided to join them.' He handed the telescope back to Nora as he spoke. 'We arrived and hiked up the mountain. It took hours walking up the steep path. We finally arrived at our campsite in the late afternoon. My mum and dad and I lay down on the grass and watched the sky as we fell asleep. The shooting stars were like white stripes against the dark sky. I have been interested in astronomy since that night.'

The three looked at the night-time sky for an hour. It was already well past midnight. They decided it was time to return to the dormitories.

The two girls used the torch to find their beds where Elsi was already asleep. Nora took off her boots and turned towards Gwen. 'Who took the painting if he didn't? Who has the most to gain?'

Gwen shrugged. 'Gwynfor is suspended, and Professor Llewellyn is the director now. He has the most to profit.'

'We should ask where he was the night of the theft,' Nora said.

---

* Water can be separated into oxygen and hydrogen through a process called electrolysis.
† Also known in English as Snowdonia National Park and Snowdon Mountain

The following day, the two asked Elsi if she had seen the professor.

'Yes. Llewellyn was at class that Friday,' said Elsi. 'I think he went to Carmarthen for dinner with his friends. I am not sure. One of our classmates saw him there.'

Gwen's hand held her chin and she spoke deliberately as she thought. 'If he went to town, there must be another suspect.'

Nora shook her head in disagreement. 'It proves nothing. He could have returned early.'

'I don't know. I'm not a detective. I'm at summer school.'

Nora took a deep breath and relaxed her shoulders. 'I want to explore the tunnels again. I saw something at the church. Besides, I like exploring tunnels. Do you want to go?'

Gwen grinned. 'Yeah, let's explore.'

They looked at Elsi with hope bubbling in their faces. She felt the excitement they shared; it was the same that night when her two friends had returned from the tunnels.

'Ok,' she said, a slight stutter betraying her fear.

They waited until after midnight, then the three girls walked through the dark residence building. Nora, holding a torch in her hand, illuminated their path. When they reached the secret door that Owain had shown them, she opened it up. Inside was quiet and dark and the night had its own personality.

They didn't speak as they entered the dark hall of the church. A few candles still burned from people who had lit them in memory of loved ones. Nora realised something as they walked to the centre aisle facing the altar. What was she doing in a church in the middle of the night? Was she really so concerned about the stolen art? She knew better. It was to prove she was breaking out of her shyness more than discovering the stolen art.

She thought about something else too. How many people came here seeking answers to their problems or to remember their deceased loved ones? Society dictates we seek answers here and repent. People had come here for hundreds of years to find answers. She imagined what their lives were like.

The girls looked at the large stained-glass window at the back of the church. The light of the moon trickled through the glass making odd shapes on the floor as they crossed over to the hall opposite the one that they had entered from the tunnel.

Nora pointed to the paintings. 'Do you notice the paintings here?'

Elsi looked at the art and then at Nora. 'What?'

'The paintings are of women.'

'So what?'

Nora gestured for them to move closer.

'Well, normally there are paintings of male saints. Paintings of females are not common. The church has been dominated by males for centuries and women were rarely portrayed. Especially these two.'

Elsi stepped closer to the oil paintings. 'What's the matter with these?'

Nora was hesitant to answer. 'This painting is of the

Greek scientist Hypatia,' she said eventually.* 'She was a teacher and scientist in the Egyptian city of Alexandria. She was murdered when her teachings went against the new religion at the time – Christianity. She died for her beliefs when her science went against what the powerful priests were preaching.'

Elsi approached the other to examine it. 'And this one?'

Gwen stepped closer to the painting. 'I think I recognise this one. It's Boudicca, the female warrior who fought against the Romans.'†

Nora took the candle in one hand before approaching the painting in slow motion. 'Let's look at it more closely.'

As she examined the brush strokes and the vibrant colours, she thought it didn't seem old. None of the paint was cracked or dirty, unlike other paintings she had seen in galleries she had visited with her parents. With her hands slightly shaking, she lifted the frame away from the wall and peered behind it. She let out a gasp. 'There it is. The missing painting! Someone has attached it to the back of the frame with nails.'

'Let me see the other one,' said Gwen. She let out a gasp too. 'Someone has nailed the third missing painting to the back of the Boudicca one.'

Nora was now fiddling with the candle, moving it back and forth between her fingers. Her voice shook as she spoke. 'What should we do? Leave it or take it?'

'No, no!' Elsi's voice raised an octave as panic started

---

* Discover more about Hypatia, and her scientific studies.
† Discover more about Boudicca, the queen of the Iceni, a Brythonic tribe who led a revolt against the Romans in ancient Britain.

to take hold of her. 'Let's leave it. Where would we take it? Who would we tell? They might blame us if someone sees us carrying them back to the residence halls.'

They looked at each other and Nora saw her own nervousness reflected in Elsi's eyes. Without a word they hurried back to the tunnels to return to their dormitory.

Nora had a plan. She wanted to talk to someone who had studied with her teachers Gwynfor and Llewellyn. So, after researching the names of the former students, she waited until after dinner and put on her black leather boots, a dark grey wool sweater and her dark blue cotton jacket, which was covered with patches she had sewn on the sleeves showing world explorers and motorcycles.

Gwen had gone home for the bank holiday weekend, so there was only Elsi remaining. She was studying at a table next to her bed when Nora approached.

'Can you come with me?' she asked hopefully. 'I am going to check something out, but I am afraid to go alone.'

'No. I can't.' Elsi was hesitant and seemed torn between her studies and the adventure her friend was promising. 'I made an enormous effort to study here. I don't want to get into trouble. Besides, I am going to visit Cardiff, the capital, tomorrow.'

Nora sighed and walked towards the door. 'Ok. I understand. It's better you don't go.' She paused and buttoned up her jacket before putting her hand on the door handle to open it.

'Wait! You can't go over the wall by yourself. It's too dangerous. I'll go with you.'

Nora smiled and hugged her friend.

It was getting late. They took the time-worn Celtic path that Owain had shown her to climb over the stone wall. The trees and bushes cast dark shadows, which danced and bobbed as the cool night breeze gently blew the branches. Nora and Elsi tried in vain to keep their thoughts from imagining that the shadows were coming alive and hurried forward until they reached the wall and climbed over. Nora's destination was just outside the school grounds at the River Towy, near the bridge.

Once they arrived, she said to Elsi, 'Stay here. It could be dangerous. If something happens, run and call the police.'

Nora walked towards the bridge near the bank of the river. She found the one she was looking for. She cleared her throat to sound confident and said, 'Kaixo.'*

The man was sitting up in his makeshift bed. He wore a wool jacket and had an open bottle of wine behind him.

She continued speaking in the Basque language. She knew he understood her words by the look on his face. 'Your name is Markel. Right?' It was more of an assertion than a question.

He looked at her, then after a few moments cleared his throat and spoke in Basque. His voice was deep and rasping. 'You are the first person in years who has asked me for my name. And in my own language too.' He grinned and adjusted his jacket. 'You must be Basque like

---

* Hello in Basque

me.' His face looked different, softer, gentler, a reflection of his younger self. 'How do you know my name?'

Nora kept her distance. 'You were a student at the school at one time, right?'

'Yes.'

'I found your name and picture at the library – from old school photos. I am Nora from Bilbao. The first time we met, you were speaking Basque at the square with the water fountain.'

He looked surprised and said, 'You were the girl from the other day who gave me the biscuits. I am from Vitoria,' he said with his head held high.

She nodded in agreement, 'Do you remember Llewellyn and Gwynfor? Tell me about them. They were bullies, right?'

'Yes, they were bullies,' Markel said in deep thought. 'They were intelligent but arrogant. They felt superior to others and laughed at other people's mistakes.'

Nora looked confused and asked, 'Gwynfor bullied Llewellyn, right? With the help of others?'

He shook his head from side to side. 'Not like that. Gwynfor did bully, but not Llewellyn. They both bullied Seren.'

Nora's eyes widened trying to make sense of what he was saying. 'Seren?'

'Yes, especially her. Isn't that ironic? The bullies are now administrators and teachers preaching about values and morals. They both liked her, but she wasn't interested in dating them. Teachers often ignored that the two boys were bullying her. They said it was mostly innocent teasing. Most of the staff were men and misogynistic. Once Gwynfor and Llewellyn knew they couldn't date her, they started calling her *walha*.'

Nora didn't understand the word. 'What does walha mean?'

'It was an Anglo-Saxon term for a stranger or an outsider. The Anglo-Saxons who invaded and established themselves in England called the people who spoke Celtic languages, like Brittonic, walha. Gwynfor and Llewellyn used the word as a weapon. She came here as a young child. Her family came from another country. Her father was a mechanical engineer in his country, but because of his status as an immigrant, he could only find work in the mines. He died because of working conditions while she was quite young. The walha word eventually became the area known as Wales.'

Everything was beginning to fit in like pieces of a puzzle. She composed herself before speaking again. 'Markel, I have to go. I have to tell someone about this.' She walked away, but stopped and asked him.

'And you?' she asked curiously. 'Did they bully you too?'

'No, no. I was a popular student. My parents split up while I was at school. It had a tremendous impact on me. I can't be angry at the world for my mistakes. I always thought I deserved better and believed that the world owed me something. The world doesn't owe me anything.'

Nora could hear the pain in his voice, and she fought back the emotion that was rising inside.

'I have broken dreams and many missed opportunities because of poor decisions.'

'I am so sorry,' Nora said. 'But I have to go. Askerrik

asko!'*

~

With her thoughts racing, she hurried back to Elsi who
was pacing up and down when she arrived. They didn't
stop to discuss what had happened but hurried back to
discuss the events of the evening in the safety of their
dormitory. When they arrived, there was a message on
the door of her room. It read, 'Meet me at the museum
ASAP - Owain.'

'I'm going to the museum to meet him. I can't ask you
to go with me again.'

Elsi sighed and nodded before sitting back down at
her study desk. 'I don't want to risk my status as a student.
Be careful and call me if you need help.'

'Ok. I will.'

Nora checked her phone. The battery was low, but
she didn't have time to charge it; who would she ring
anyway? But she decided not to take the tunnels by
herself and went to meet Owain. From a dark window in
Crymu Hall, a figure stood watching her going to the
museum.

'Hey! You finally came,' said Owain. He was relieved
and it showed on his face. 'What a place to meet. What's
up? Did you find out anything?'

'What are you talking about?' Nora was confused. 'I
got a message that you wanted to meet me here.'

---

* Thank you very much in the Basque language

'I didn't leave you any message. The teachers took our phones away in class. I didn't get the chance to get it back yet. I found a message in my mailbox that you wanted to show me something urgently.'

They heard the sound of the main door opening and both looked at each other.

'Who can that be?' Owain whispered.

'Probably the person who left us the messages. We've got to hide. Let's go.'

The darkness of the museum added to an already tense moment, and as the moonlight filtered through the stained-glass windows, it gave the museum an eerie dancing light. As if this wasn't enough, the wind outside beat against the doors as if knocking to come in.

They hurried to the nearest hall. It was dark and smelled of years of old furniture polish and dust. They ran down to hide behind a bookcase.

Nora looked around. 'Where is the secret passage?'

Owain pressed his back against the wall. 'I think it is on the other side, close to a gallery of paintings. It's too late to go now. Be quiet.'

They both heard footsteps getting closer and a light from a torch getting brighter.

They held their breath and squeezed each other's hands. The figure stopped at the entrance and shined the light down the hall. An icy chill ran up and down Nora's spine. They heard a loud bang of a door. The figure turned and rushed towards the sound.

Nora exhaled. 'Let's go.'

'No, no way. Let's stay here. Maybe the person won't come back.'

'Are you kidding me? We have to move. The person

might come back. Now's our chance. It's like hide and seek. The longer we stay in one spot, the more likely they will find us.'

They heard a loud bang and metal bars dragging. They looked at the door to see it closed and the gate down.

'The person must have left and locked the door,' Nora gasped.

He twisted his head to look around. 'Perhaps they got scared when the wind closed the door.'

She checked her phone, but the battery was dead. 'Did you see the person?'

'No. I was too scared to look. And you?'

'No. I couldn't turn my head to look.'

They walked towards the main entrance. Owain cried out, 'The gate is locked! The museum is closed until Tuesday. It's Friday. We'll be trapped for four days.' His panic was infectious, so Nora took in deep breaths to stay calm herself.

'The secret entrance,' Nora almost whispered in her response. But the hidden entrance was down a short dark corridor, and the gate was closed. 'This gate looks old, possibly centuries old, but maybe ...'

She looked around. 'I have an idea. Take some of this construction material, the long metal pole and a few cement blocks. Let's make a lever. Do you remember what Llewellyn said about the scientist Archimedes? The ancient scholar said with a long pole and a block, he could lift the world.' Nora looked hopeful. 'It's the same principle. We use the metal pole as leverage to break the lock that has been there for centuries.'

He nodded his agreement, and soon they had

collected all the items together that they needed. First, they put one long metal pole vertically into a small hole in the floor. Then, they took another metal pole and put it horizontally between the gate and the lock. Finally, they crossed the vertical pole with a horizontal one and pushed to get leverage. After a short while, they managed to pry the rusty gate open.

Owain dropped the heavy pole to the ground. 'Learning ancient history actually helps. I never liked history before now. I never saw the point of it. It was all about reading about dead people.'

Nora didn't reply. 'Let's go to church. Whoever trapped us here is probably going to move the stolen paintings. It's the thief's best chance to move it. It's dark, a long weekend and they think they trapped us.'

'Is it up to us to stop the person? Shouldn't we go back to the residency to tell someone? I've had enough of this already.'

'Who will we tell?' Nora said firmly. 'We don't know for sure who the person is. How do we explain what we have been doing here? I am not saying that we have to confront the person. That is too dangerous. We can take the painting or see the person taking it. Besides, it's raining and windy and it's a long walk to the church.'

Owain grunted, 'What are we waiting for? Come on.'

The church, through the tunnel, wasn't far away and it didn't take long to reach it. Nora wasn't sure whether the thief would go to take the painting, but she thought now offered the best opportunity. It was a chance she had to take. They held their breath as the hidden door to the church creaked open. Soon they were in the hall standing amongst the discarded statues. They crept, like shadows, past the altar to the opposite hall. The paintings were still there! Finding a hiding spot in the pulpit, they positioned themselves so they had a good view of the church and waited. It wasn't long before they heard the entrance door scraping across the stone floor. A beam of torchlight entered, followed by a figure. It was too far away to see the person's face as they watched them walk to the hall that contained the stolen paintings.

Nora whispered, 'We can trap the person like they trapped us with the iron gate.'

'Sounds good. Why don't we sound the church bells as well?'

'Ok, I'll close the gate and you ring the bells, then we'll meet at the door and run. The noise will attract someone's attention.'

'Come on, let's go!' Owain said as he went silently to the control panel that was next to the pulpit.

Nora tiptoed to the opening of the hall where the gate stood open. Peering inside, a person stood facing the paintings on the wall. Nora paused for a moment gathering together the courage to grab the old iron gate to pull it shut. The sound of the lock as she closed it rang out in the silence. The mysterious person turned at the sound. It was Seren! Her mouth dropped in surprise, and she spoke, but Nora didn't wait to hear what she was going to say. She ran towards the main door, reaching it just when the church bells rang twelve times.

It wasn't long before the sound of the church bells had attracted the campus security, the grounds crew and the night staff. They found Seren in the church behind the closed gates. The police were called and questioned her about what she was doing, but she stayed quiet and refused to talk about her reasons for going into the building in the middle of the night. Despite her reluctance to speak, the police discovered that she too had been a student and they surmised that she probably knew about the passages. Eventually, the police concluded that she had wanted revenge after being bullied as a young student and took the paintings to get Gwynfor and Llewellyn in trouble.

During the last week of school, Elsi told Gwen and Nora what she heard a teacher say as they sat outside after class. 'Llewellyn mentioned in his class that it was more of a crime of passion than theft.'

Gwen looked puzzled. 'What did he mean, crime of passion?'

Nora explained in more detail. 'Envy, rage, jealousy and, in this case, revenge led to the theft. It wasn't for profit.'

Gwen frowned. 'It's so sad. I liked her as a teacher, and she was passionate about art.'

During the last remaining few days of school, Nora walked into her dormitory, a big smile on her face and her hand raised in the air. She waved the paper she was holding to attract her friends' attention. 'I have tickets to the museum. Owain and the others are going. Do you want to go?' she asked excitedly.

'Well, no, not really,' Gwen said in a low voice. 'I want

to go to the Llyn Peninsula to the beach. To be honest, the museum is boring for me. It is just a lot of old things from the past. We learn nothing from it. At the beach, we can bring sandwiches and go for a swim.'

'I like the beach as well, to swim or look for shells,' said Nora with a hint of pain in her voice, 'but the group of students are going to the museum now.'

Nora turned to Elsi. 'What about you?'

'Well...' Elsi looked down. 'I want to go to the beach too before I return to Peru. I want to have fun.'

'Ok,' replied Nora with a disappointed sigh. As the two turned away, Nora crossed her arms and watched them leave. She got a feeling that her friendship wouldn't be the same. She started thinking that life is a continuous change. As she walked to the door, holding the museum tickets, she knew there would be more changes to come.

PART II

Seventeen-year-old Nora O'Brien Pacheco had just come back to Bilbao, Spain. She had finished her two-month summer studies in Wales and had a few weeks before school started again.

Her mother greeted her at the airport with a big hug and kiss. Nora looked around and asked, 'Where's Papi?'

'You know he's always doing something,' her mother replied with a warm smile. 'You can talk to him later. He has gone to an appointment.' She put her arm around Nora and pulled her close to her.

Nora frowned. 'Ok.'

It disappointed her that her father hadn't come to pick her up. On the way home, she told her mother stories about her studies in Wales, and her mother listened with interest and happiness that she had gained so much from the visit. When she had finished her stories she said, 'I want to go to Ainhoa's house to tell her about my trip.' Earlier in the day, she had written to her best friend to meet.

As soon as she got home, she went straight to Ainhoa's house, where they hugged at the front door. Nora smelt a slight odour of cigarettes on her breath.

'Hey, tell me all about your Welsh trip,' Ainhoa said with excitement. They went to her bedroom to talk more. Nora talked about her classmates and what happened to the stolen art. She smiled excitedly and looked down when she mentioned Owain.

'I have got news too,' Ainhoa said with a wide smile. 'I have a boyfriend!'

Nora's mouth opened and she raised her eyebrows. Ainhoa was timid and self-conscious, like her, but she was happy for her friend.

'Who is he?'

'It's Aitor, the boy who hangs out at the plaza.'

'Aitor?' Nora said with a questioning look. 'The boy from the lost ones?'* She said it naturally, with no sarcasm.

'I don't like using that word anymore. They're nice. You should go with me to meet them. I was bored when you and Olatz left on holiday. I walked my dog a lot. I would see them sometimes. Then Iruni called me over whilst walking my dog.'

'Iruni?' Nora asked in a doubtful tone.

'Yes. Iruni. Do you remember her? She was in primary school with us and now she is in our science

---

* The lost ones are a group of teenage boys and girls who have no direction in life. They spend their days walking their aggressive dogs, riding scooters and hanging out at the parks.

class. You will like her. She has a forceful personality. She doesn't let anyone mess with her. That's where I met Aitor. I was quiet at first. They were always talking about their dogs or motorbikes, or football teams. Aitor took notice of me, and we started talking.

'I remember him in primary school. He was chubby and quiet.'

Ainhoa gasped. 'He dropped out of secondary school last year to follow his dreams. Come with me. Come on. You'll like it. It was weird at first because we saw them as lost and never going to do anything. Now I know them and they're so nice.'

Nora was unsure that she wanted to. 'Ok, I will, but not now. I want to go home to see my father. I want to tell him about my trip.'

'Ok, I'll call you later,' Ainhoa said.

They hugged and Nora went home.

Nora walked home from Ainhoa's house. As she walked through her front door, Nora heard her mother talking to her father in their bedroom. She ran to their room, excited to see him. As she entered, her mother stood with her hand on her father's forehead. He was lying down. She paused at the foot of the bed, her mouth dropping open as she looked at him. Was it her father? He looked so different, so thin and his eyes were red. What's more, his hair was cropped short, and it had turned completely grey; she also noticed patches missing.

'Papi, what's wrong?' she asked in a panic.

He looked at her with a weak smile. 'I'm sick. I have prostate cancer.'

'What is prostate cancer?' she said in disbelief. 'I know from classes at school that it's dangerous, but I never gave it much attention.'

Her father explained. 'Your body comprises millions of cells. They all have a function. Some are to maintain your skin; others are to help your organs work properly and thousands of others to keep your body healthy. Some of these cells, over time, get corrupted and stop doing their job. They mutate and start attacking your body. It naturally wants to multiply, and it's spread by your glands. Once it gets into other parts of the body, it's harder to treat.' He looked glum and in pain. 'It has already spread to my organs.'

She sat down at the foot of his bed; her legs felt heavy and weak.

Her father continued, 'I go to chemotherapy to slow the cancer growth. I take medication to keep the pain away, but I am incoherent and remember nothing. The pain is too intense when I am off it. I didn't take the medication today so I could talk to you.'

'When did you know?'

'They diagnosed me last year before our holiday in Wales.'

'Is that why you sent me off to Wales?'

'No, not exactly,' her mother said. 'We wanted you to become more independent and to make accommodations for your father.'

He sighed with a far-off look. 'There were so many books I wanted to read. I wanted to visit many places with you. My next destination was South America, to Machu Picchu.'

The news about the cancer had twisted Nora's stomach in knots and she was feeling queasy.

Her mother interrupted and said, 'Let's talk later with Papi. I'll come out to talk to you in a minute, dear.'

Nora didn't wait for her mother to talk. She went to her bedroom and looked up prostate cancer on her phone. As she read more about it, she bit her fingernails until they couldn't go any shorter. *Why didn't the world stop to focus on her father's illness? Doesn't everyone want to help her solve her problem?*

A few days later, she went out to meet with her friend Ainhoa and her new friends at the plaza. There were between four to eight of them most of the time, but people came and left the group at various times. Most of the boys wore earrings, sometimes more than one in each ear. They valued strength and had aggressive dogs to match their personality. Standing there with the boys was their friend Olatz. She was the most beautiful. Tall and slender, she had matured earlier than the rest of the girls, and many of the boys took notice of her.

The girl speaking was Iruni. She was of medium height, with black hair, a black leather jacket and large hoop earrings. She had a rough beauty about her. As Nora and Ainhoa walked up to the group, Iruni raised her voice to one of the boys.

'Where have you been?' she said to Eneko. 'I have

been calling you and you didn't pick up and then you turned off your phone. You don't do that.'

Eneko smirked. 'Los Jardines de Albia Park.'

'Los Jardines de Albia Park?' she snapped. 'Yeah right! You can fool others, but not me. You don't know me well enough to think you can lie. I don't believe it.'

'Why are you so angry?' Eneko said sarcastically. 'Did you miss me and start talking about us to your friends?'

'No way! I have other friends. My world doesn't revolve around you. You said that we were going to meet, and you didn't show up. Come on, girls,' Iruni commanded, 'let's go for a walk!'

Like soldiers, the girls got up and followed her.

'Do you want a cigarette?' Iruni asked Nora.

Nora shook her head. 'No thanks.'

'It's probably for the best. I started smoking with my first boyfriend who smoked. We didn't last long. He was so immature, hot headed and was more interested in his dogs than me. He would often call me at night to talk and he would use a different tone of voice than the one he used in front of his friends. Like his friends, he wanted to fix his motorbikes but didn't know how to do it. They once took his motorcycle apart but couldn't get it back together.' She laughed. 'My ex was so angry! His mother had to pay a mechanic to put it back together. Then he trained his dogs. He didn't work because he wanted his freedom to pursue his hobbies, but he didn't have the money to do anything. For him and his friends, going to the next neighbourhood is like going to a foreign country. He would never hang out at Los Jardines of Albia. It's too public to hang out to smoke. They are going to live and die in this neighbourhood. I don't want that life. That's why I'm still in school. Even though it's boring, I don't want to end up like them.'

Nora admired Iruni's confidence, and she compared herself with her new friend; she felt that what she had to say wasn't important to others. Even though she knew the topic better than the rest, she stayed quiet. When she tried to speak, her mouth and brain would freeze.

After hanging out at the plaza, she returned home. Her mother worked full time and then took care of her father, and Nora could see exhaustion consuming her. Although her father could get around the house on his own, she knew her mother would never stop helping him. Nora, at first, hoped that modern medicine and technology could cure cancer. However, she noticed he was weaker as the weeks passed. He began sleeping more, and when she helped him get up, his once firm body was becoming like a sponge.

One day after school, Ainhoa knocked on Nora's door. Nora was expecting her since they had texted each other early in the day, but her friend wasn't alone. Iruni was with her.

Nora's mother greeted them at the door. 'Hi, Iruni!' Nora's mother said. 'It has been a long time. I remember you were in primary school. You were so cute! How's your mum?'

'She's ok,' Iruni responded, with flushed skin.

The three girls walked to Nora's bedroom. Iruni's face lit up. 'Wow! You have a cool bedroom. I like the world map. Did you travel to all these places?'

'Some places I have already been to and the others I plan to go to with my parents in the future.'

Finally, someone other than her parents had commented about her room, she thought. No one besides Ainhoa and Olatz had been there, so it was good to show her bedroom to someone she admired. Her bedroom showed off a side of her personality that was normally hidden to most people.

'Look at all your books!' Iruni said with a surprised look. 'I enjoy reading non-fiction books about psychology. Antiques! I like antiques too.' She touched some of the objects. 'I buy antiques and sell them to the temple priest to make money.'

Ainhoa and Nora watched as she examined the bedroom.

Nora spoke up. 'My father got most of them for me. He likes going to flea markets too or second-hand shops. It's fun looking for an old object that needs to be saved.'

Just then Nora's mother called, 'Nora, can you help me for a minute?'

A male voice screamed as dishes crashed to the floor. Ainhoa and Iruni looked at each other.

Nora looked at them and blushed as she shouted to her mother. 'Ok, I am coming.'

It was becoming clear that it was getting more and more difficult to help her father. He got angry when they wouldn't let him walk. He wanted to have a strong male around, saying that his wife and daughter weren't strong enough to meet his needs. Her father had no family near him because he had immigrated over twenty-five years ago and the only family he had was his daughter and wife. He became confused and got a medical condition called sundowning, a condition where his sleep cycle changed. He started sleeping during the day and staying up all night.

Later that night, after Nora's friends had left, Nora fell asleep early.

'Michael. Where are you?' A familiar voice woke Nora in the middle of the night. 'Do you still have my rock-n-roll records? I want to go to Durkin Park.'

Nora rushed into her father's bedroom and asked, 'What Papi? It's me, Nora. Durkin Park? Do you mean La Salve Park?'

He started screaming at her. 'I want Michael! Where is Michael?'

She touched his arm, and he turned his head and stared at her. 'Valentina, let me go with you to walk in Recoleta.' He grabbed her hand.

'Papi. It's me.' His grip was tightening, and Nora's panic worsened.

Her father blinked and his confusion fell away; he recognised his daughter once more. 'Help me, Nora. My legs are so painful. They are burning.'

Her mother walked in half asleep to see what the commotion was about. Since her husband's illness she had been sleeping in the spare bedroom so she could go to work in the morning; even so, her eyes were bloodshot with tiredness. They gave him water and stayed with him until he fell asleep.

'We'll talk in the morning,' her mother whispered. Nora heard the strain in her mother's voice.

The following morning, her mother said to Nora, 'I know with your father sick, you want to help him as much as possible, but you have to continue with your life. We can't lay in bed the whole day depressed.'

Nora agreed and wanted to understand what had happened the previous night.

Her mother explained. 'Durkin Park is in Chicago, where he lived. You have been too. We have pictures of you there.'

'He asked for Michael,' Nora said.

'You probably don't remember him. Michael is his brother. You met him when you were four years old. He played with you all the time and you followed him like a puppy.'

He had never mentioned his past life or his country in her seventeen years of life.

'Who is Valentina?'

'Valentina must have been a good friend,' her mother said as she changed the subject. 'His episodes are getting worse. He needs help to go to the toilet and take a bath. We have to talk.' Nora's mother spoke with a serious tone. 'I want to know what you think. We can hire a lady to take care of him at home or...' with a slight hesitation in her voice, 'we can put him in a home that has help around the clock.'

'No, no, no.' Nora's eyes welled up with tears. 'Don't send Papi away. He has to stay here. I will help more.'

'You have too many other responsibilities. You have school and homework. He would be so disappointed if you started doing poorly in your classes. It's more affordable to hire a lady to watch him.'

Nora wiped her eyes. 'How about two helpers? I think one lady for eight hours is too much for one person. We can go to an agency or ask our friends if they know someone who can help. How about four hours a day for each caretaker? They can rotate in the morning.'

Her mother smiled in agreement.

The following day at school, Nora approached her friend Ainhoa and said, 'It was nice of you to bring Iruni to my house. I wasn't expecting it.'

'It wasn't my idea to bring her over. She called me first and suggested we go together to your house to visit you.'

'She wanted to go to my house?'

'Yeah, I wanted to go to the square to see what Aitor was doing, but she wanted to call you first. I think she was curious about you.'

Nora stopped and looked at Ainhoa. 'Hey, about my father; keep it quiet. Ok? I don't want anyone knowing about it.'

'Of course.'

Later on, at school between classes, Nora went to the main office to enquire about scholarships and study abroad options for the coming year. Even though she knew that with her father ill, she wouldn't leave until he was healthy. She talked with her teacher Eskarne and her teacher told her to come back after school to discuss her options more fully. As she turned around, Iruni was standing there as if listening from a few feet away.

'Hey, what's up?' Nora asked, unable to hide her surprise.

'Not much,' answered Iruni. 'I am just looking at the coming events at school. Come on, let's go to the park after school and hang out. I have something to show you.'

'Well, I don't know. I have to come back here for something.'

'Don't worry, it will be here when you come back.' She took Nora's hand and pulled her away. 'Come on, let's go!'

On their way out the school door, Ainhoa was waiting for them and together they went to the plaza.

'Hey, we want to sell some antiques to the temple priest, to make some money,' Iruni said excitedly. 'Do you want to come?'

'The temple priest?' Nora asked. 'Father De La Torre?'

Ainhoa shook her head. 'No, no, he's been gone for some time. It's Father Icono now.'

'He buys low and sells high,' Iruni said, frowning. 'Anyway, I got this brass lamp that I bought at the flea market for five euros to sell to the priest.'

'And I am going to sell some of my bug and fossil collection,' Ainhoa added. 'It's so silly to keep it.'

Ainhoa's statement about her fossil collection surprised Nora. She knew how much Ainhoa loved her fossils.

Iran turned towards Nora. 'Do you have anything to sell?'

'Well, I haven't thought about it. I have a few things, maybe my shark tooth and bug collection.'

Ainhoa interjected. 'Think about it. You don't have to sell it if you don't want to, but why not take it along to see what price you can get then decide if you want to sell it or not. Besides, we are not going until we get more antiques to sell.'

Later that week, during school, the teacher, Eskarne, walked up to Nora. She was plain-spoken and serious.

'There were only a few scholarship applications available to study abroad,' she said to Nora. 'Your friend Iruni got the last application. She came in the following morning when you enquired about scholarships. There is limited aid. Otherwise, everybody would ask for it and the universities would receive thousands of enquiries. It would be impossible to sort out. I was surprised,' Eskarne said with raised eyebrows. 'She has decent marks, but she doesn't speak English. She stopped studying at the English academy to hang out with her friends. It is first come first served. Why didn't you come back when you said you would?'

Nora grunted and crossed her arms. 'I was busy.'

'Nora,' said Eskarne with a disappointed tone, 'you seem to be a little more disrespectful lately. It's a difficult situation with your father. You should think about yourself. I think Iruni is only out for herself. She may be envious. Make yourself number one. You have an option to take a written exam to apply for scholarships to study abroad.'

Nora had never heard of that option and asked, 'How many students choose the written exam?'

'Well, writing is difficult. From what I can remember, no one has ever chosen the written exam option. If you want to take it, the deadline is in March. I wouldn't wait until the last minute. Think about it.'

Over the following months, Nora accompanied her father to his chemotherapy sessions and started helping her mother, whenever she could, with his medical needs.

One day, her father opened his eyes and looked around. He frowned. 'I want to go back home now. I don't want to be here in a stranger's house.'

Nora looked perplexed. 'We are at home.'

Her father looked at her in a state of confusion. 'No, I want to return to my house. Who are these strangers?'

'They are the carers who help you,' Nora said. Her voice cracked as she struggled to disguise the distress she felt. 'They have been with you for a few months now.'

'I don't need help. I want to go home to Durkin Park.'

'What, Papi? You are home, and they are your carers.'

'No, I want to go to Durkin Park!'

'Papi, the van is coming to pick you up for your sessions.'

Tears appeared in his eyes. 'Nora, take me back to my bedroom. I don't want to go anywhere. Don't let anyone inside my bedroom. I want to be alone. Call my brother, Michael, as well. Tell him I need help.'

Nora stared at him wide eyed and didn't know what to say. She told the driver that he wasn't well and that they had a doctor's appointment tomorrow.

The following day, at the hospital, the doctor took her father's pulse and checked his other vitals. When he had finished, he beckoned Nora and her mother to follow him into the hallway. His expression was solemn as he spoke to them.

'When your father started chemo, he weighed eighty-seven kilos. Now he is sixty kilos. He has deteriorated too much and probably has only a few days to live. We want to admit him to the hospice now. You should be with him.'

Nora and her mother walked slowly back into the hospital room. Their heads hung low, and they had no words to say to each other. Her father's eyes were closed, and his breathing was shallow and gasping. From time to time, he would open his eyes and stare into the distance, as if remembering another time and place. He mumbled in English, but his words were incoherent. His hand trembled and she grabbed it to comfort him, nearly dropping it again when she realised how much he had worsened in the last three months.

Hours passed and a stream of doctors and nurses started coming and going. At first, they hurried about their tasks, but after a little while, one of the doctors shook his head to the nurse, and she leaned forward to plump up her father's pillow and straighten the sheet around him before leaving the room.

This wasn't how it was supposed to be. Nora wasn't ready to watch her father die, but she stood next to her father's bed whilst her mother whispered to him as he passed away.

'Mum,' Nora said, her eyes red and puffy from the tears she had shed on the way home, 'can people tell when they are going to die? Papi wanted to stay in his bedroom by himself yesterday.'

'I don't know. Sick people may feel too weak to

continue living. People who are religious would say their soul is leaving. Others, who are not religious, would say they are slipping away... It's been a long day. Let's get some rest.'

Her mother took her in her arms, and they hugged and let the tears tumble down their faces.

Nora had missed more time in school than she ever had before. Weeks had passed since her father's death, and she had not wanted to leave her home, but eventually she ventured out and met with her friends at Plaza Moraza.

'Her father died,' one of the lost ones whispered as she approached.

'That old guy was her father?' Eneko asked in a low voice. 'We used to see him walking all the time. I thought he was her grandfather.'

The other boys laughed, hiding their faces with their hands. Nora glared at them. She looked at Ainhoa for support. Her friend didn't speak and put her head down. Nora didn't know what to do: to say something or stand there and pretend it wasn't a big deal. She just stood motionless, her arms crossed over her chest.

It was Iruni who shouted at the boys, 'Hey, shut up! That's rude!'

With the tension broken, Nora said in a weak voice, 'I have to go back home.'

'I'll come with you,' a red faced Ainhoa replied as she got up and walked with Nora.

Nora's face was twisted as she said to Ainhoa, 'I can't

believe Iruni would mention my father to the rest of them.'

She looked at Nora and dropped her eyes down. 'She didn't. I did.'

Nora looked at her best friend in disbelief.

Ainhoa continued, 'I am so sorry that I mentioned it. I told Aitor and he told everyone else. I wanted his attention, so I told him, hoping that he would look up from his phone and talk with me. He just walked away without paying me any attention. That's when he told his friends. I was angry that he did, and I went home. Later that night, he called me and said how much he missed me. It's so nice when he pays attention to me.'

Nora frowned, but she looked up and said, 'You are my best friend. We all have to learn to forgive and forget.' She stepped forward and hugged her friend.

It was a week after the incident at the plaza. 'Take this!' Iruni commanded Nora and Ainhoa while they were at school for lunch. She gave them eggs. 'Put your school bags next to mine and come with me.'

Nora froze. 'What are you doing?'

'You'll see,' she answered with a smirk. 'You've been avoiding us for a week now and a lot has happened.'

They walked outside the school grounds to the street. The teachers parked their cars in front of the school.

'I want to egg this teacher's car,' she sneered. He gave me a poor mark on my exam and said he was going to call my mum.'

Nora gasped. 'What? No way! I am not doing it!'

'Ok, fine.'

They started to walk back to the school's entrance when Iruni suddenly turned and threw the egg, hitting the car on the window. All three girls hurried back to the school entrance.

'Hey, keep going,' Iruni said. 'I'll catch up in a minute.'

They entered the front door feeling stunned by what had happened. A teacher walking down the corridor noticed that Nora and Ainhoa were carrying eggs. She stopped them to ask what they were doing. The two girls wanted to explain they were carrying them for Iruni, but when they looked back, Iruni was not in sight.

Nora's teacher, Eskarne, found Nora before school finished and took her to the office to talk. As they sat down, students and teachers were busy leaving school. Nora's stomach twisted in knots and her mouth became dry.

'A teacher said someone threw an egg at his car. Did you have anything to do with it?'

'I didn't throw the egg.'

'Do you know who did it?'

There was a long silence. 'I'd rather not say.'

Eskarne sighed. 'Ok. I'll have to call your mother and Ainhoa's mum as well. Are you still keeping busy after school? Are you still taking art classes?'

'I'd rather hang out with my friends. I don't see much value in art.'

'You don't know the power of art?

'What can art do?'

'Let me tell you something. When I was a little girl around 1995, my mother used to take me along to do errands around Bilbao and sometimes we would walk along the river. Bilbao was a lot different back then. It was known as an industrial town for ship building. Closed down factories, dirty river water, and civil unrest made the city unattractive. There was a lot of debate about building the Guggenheim Museum.* Only people who lived here and witnessed the change can appreciate the decision. A museum of art helped transform the city. It wasn't only the museum, there were other decisions that made Bilbao a cosmopolitan city that it is. The metro opened around 1995, they cleaned the river and tore down old factories. Don't be afraid to make decisions. It's empowering to be able to make them, especially if you make the right ones. It will make you confident.'

As Nora was getting up, she turned to look at her teacher. 'Is it too late to take the written essay?'

Eskarne collected paperwork off the table. 'No. Go to the government office that handles the request for scholarships. Then you have a month to write it.'

Nora's mother received a phone call to go to school to talk about Nora's behaviour. They found eggs in her school bag and the teacher saw her carrying an egg in her hand.

'Nora?' her mother asked. 'I can't believe it.'

Eskarne met with Nora's mother to talk about the incident. 'Well,' said her teacher, 'she got into trouble and some of her marks slipped as well. It's easy to blame the

---

* Source BBC Arts-The Bilbao effect: How 20 years of Gehry's Guggenheim transformed the city. William Cook, 16 October 2017.

girls that she's hanging out with, but it's not that easy. She makes her own decisions. Do me a favour and don't be so harsh with her. Don't discipline and try taking away her rights by not letting her out. That has the opposite effect. Keep on having open conversations and talk with her every day. When you see something suspicious, point it out without yelling at her.'

Nora's mother fidgeted. 'Then what?'

'Keep your fingers crossed. You never know how someone will turn out as an adult. I have seen plenty of students. Some surprised me and others disappointed me. You know their friends are an enormous influence on them. Within five years, they'll probably never ever see the same friends again due to life circumstances. They are very sensitive at this age, especially about their appearance. They think being beautiful is everything, and if you mention something negative about it, that may affect their self-esteem. I don't think Nora is one of those who attaches herself to beauty, but she may be influenced by other things.'

As Nora left the school, Iruni and Ainhoa were waiting for her.

'Oh, man, that was so close,' Iruni said wryly. 'I saw the teacher talking with you, so I went the other way. What happened to you?'

Nora glared at her. 'Not much. Eskarne called my mum.'

'That's it! I knew it. A nice girl never gets punished. Anyway, do you remember we were going to sell antiques to the temple priest? Let's get our antiques and make some money for the weekend.'

When Nora arrived home, she went to her father's bedroom and looked around. He, too, had a map on the wall. She looked at it and looked at a pin inserted in Peru, his next destination. She laid down on his bed and remembered him.

Shortly afterwards, her mother arrived home from the meeting at school. She was worried about the direction her daughter was taking. She told Nora what Eskarne had told her.

'You also stopped going to art class this year,' her mother said. 'If you always follow people, you will always be last. Do you remember the poster that your father placed in your bedroom? Find your way, take chances, be authentic, be bold. Think about what he taught you.'

Later that week, Nora went to the government building to enquire about scholarships.

'Hi,' she said, 'I want an application for the scholarship to study abroad, please.'

'Your ID please.' The man behind the desk was bored. He picked up her ID and studied it, frowning as he did so. 'That's an interesting name that you have.'

'My father gave it to me in memory of his mother.' Nora replied. 'He wasn't from here, but I was born here in Bilbao.'

'How interesting. Here is your application. Good luck.'

'Thank you. Bye.'

During the week, the three friends collected their antiques to sell. On their way to the temple priest's church, Iruni looked at them and wrinkled up her nose. 'We look silly carrying these pieces,' she said as she swung the old lamp in her hand upwards to emphasise her point.

Ainhoa opened her big bag. 'Let's put them in a school bag.'

They carried on walking towards the church's office. Before they entered, Iruni explained the selling process to her friends.

'When you sell something, you can't be desperate to sell it too cheaply. If you don't like the price, just walk away. It all depends on how desperate you are for money. It also helps to know how valuable it is. For example, is it metal? What kind? With most precious metals, a magnet doesn't stick. Don't be nice! When they see someone timid, they love it. They'll take advantage of your niceness and assume you are gullible, or naive.'

She put her arm out and stopped Nora and Ainhoa to explain further. 'When I come here with Aitor or Eneko, they don't know what they have and sell it so cheap. They find it at their grandparents' house. They have no respect.' Iruni hissed her comment and spat on the ground. All they can think about is having a few euros for the weekend. Their grandparents' possessions are being sold for nothing. It makes me sick. Listen! You never accept the first offer. You haggle! If you don't haggle, they see you as a fool. No one is getting over me. No one!'

The church was built in a typical Spanish gothic style, with large sandstone blocks and a large bell that sat on its pinnacle.

Icono, the priest, was short and wide, with a large green cloak that he also wore for mass. He had expensive rings on his fingers and a large gold cross around his neck. Looking like a medieval monk, he was bald on top, with hair on the side and back of his head.

'Well, it's good to see you again, Iruni. You are becoming a steady customer. What can I do for you today?' asked the priest.

Now it was her turn. 'I have something to sell.' Her voice was calm and steady as she pulled out the brass lamp from Ainhoa's backpack.

'How much?' came the priest's anxious reply as his eyes widened with excitement.

'I want sixty euros.'

The priest laughed. 'Everybody wants all the money in the world.'

For all her faults, Iruni was no dummy. She knew he would haggle. She started at a higher price, but she held her ground. 'I'll drop to fifty.'

He looked at her. 'I'll give you twenty euros. Money doesn't grow on trees.'

'No. I'll take forty,' she said firmly. 'It's an easy sell. Someone will buy it fast.'

Nora could tell that she knew what she was doing.

'I'll tell you what I want,' Iruni said. 'Give me that ring and twenty-five euros for the lamp.'

She picked the most expensive ring in the glass display case, knowing that the priest would never agree with her. She actually wanted the other right next to it.

'That ring cost more than you can pay. Look, I'll give you this other ring and twenty euros for the lamp.'

'Ok.' She sounded like she was selling for less than she wanted.

Next it was Ainhoa's turn. 'I have a bug collection with the guide that has the list of bugs and their description.' She hesitated as she spoke, unsure of herself.

Icono looked at it closely. 'Very interesting,' he said. 'It's a shame that these bugs are extinct or will be extinct soon. Unfortunately, no one really cares about bugs. I'll give you twenty-five euros for it.'

She glanced at Iruni to confirm or deny the offer. With a slight nod of encouragement from her friend, Ainhoa said, 'I'll take thirty euros.'

'Done!' said Icono.

They all looked at Nora.

'How about you? Do you want to sell something?' Iruni asked.

She shook her head. 'I'm not sure. I'd better not. It belonged to my father.'

They walked towards the bus stop, laughing about Iruni's audaciousness.

'Let's ask these boys at the bus stop to pay for our bus ride home,' she said.

She walked up to the boys and told them they had no money and needed to go to visit their grandmother's house. The boys, about the same age as the girls, looked at each other and agreed. She talked to them on the bus while Nora and Ainhoa sat quietly, listening to her.

The girls were getting off the bus when Iruni stopped to talk to one boy. He pulled out his phone. She walked back to her friends, who were waiting for her at the bus stop.

'I gave them Olatz's phone number!' She said with a laugh. 'She's always taking selfies of herself and posting them on her social accounts. It will surprise her when they call her!'

The following week, Nora went to see Eskarne about filling out the scholarship application.

Nora asked her teacher, 'What makes you part of a society? Is it where you are born? If you speak the language? Or have a proper name?'

Eskarne nodded and said, 'Traditional immigration to the Basque Country has been inside Spain, especially from Andalusia, Extremadura and Galicia. They came looking for work. Now, there are large numbers of immigrants from outside the country. Their children were born here, but they often hold on to their culture while adapting to a new one. Many countries with strong economies face the same challenges on how to adapt to immigration. I suppose, like any country, there will always be immigration for economic reasons, simply to find a better life. Anyway...' She said with a smile, 'let's review the application. I hope you get accepted.'

She thanked her teacher and went home to finish filling in the application.

The following day, Iruni called Nora on her phone. 'Hey, what are you doing?'

'I am studying,' answered Nora.

'Studying? Who studies at the weekend? Ainhoa is crying. She needs us.'

'Why? What happened?'

'She and Aitor had an argument. Come on! We're at the Plaza Moraza. We need to cheer her up.'

When Nora arrived, Iruni and Ainhoa were sitting on a bench in the middle of the plaza. Her best friend looked upset and had been crying. She was wearing a short black dress and large hoop earrings. Her clothes looked awkward on her. She wasn't wearing her glasses either.

'He doesn't respect you,' Iruni told Ainhoa. 'The way he talks to you. He never pays you any attention. He doesn't even look at you while you speak to him because he's always on his mobile.'

Ainhoa dried her tears. 'He goes out with his friends and only calls me when he is feeling lonely.'

'He's a guy!' Iruni said in frustration. 'What do you expect?'

'I know he's good. If I can just change him.'

'Where were you going? To a party?' Nora asked. 'Why are you dressed up?'

'I dressed up to look good. I was going to hang out with Aitor until he went up to Artxanda, but I can't walk up the mountain in high heels. I thought he would like the way I look. Look around! It's everywhere. On TV and in magazines. All you see are tall, light skinned beautiful women. That's how we're supposed to look. Every time I look at the magazines for the latest fashions, I become more depressed than happy. I don't like reading girl's magazines anymore.'

'He thinks he deserves better,' added Iruni. 'He is

fooling himself. Look at him! He is unkempt, unshaven and has no job. You can do much better.'

'He's the first boy who talked to me.' Ainhoa wiped her eyes with the back of her hand.

Iruni turned to Nora. 'Have you ever liked anyone?'

'Well, yeah.'

'Come on! Who?'

'There was a boy, Owain, that I met in Wales. I only hung out with him the last week of school.'

'Did you tell him?'

'No.'

'Did you try to keep in touch?'

'No,' said Nora, raising her voice. 'I thought about it, but...'

Iruni raised her hand in impatience. 'But what?'

'I couldn't.'

'Ha! The cat's got your tongue? So, look at me. I asked a few boys to hang out. Some of them are scared. They don't know how to talk. The shy ones always say no. The more confident ones talk to me, even though they talk a lot of trash. Why do all the shy ones think they are unique and that no one understands how special they are?' Iruni shrugged her shoulders and raised her hands, palm up, in the air. 'My sister is the same way. She's always listening, never able to say anything and always looks for the right moment to speak. Then, when the moment passes, she plays it out in her head a thousand times. What she really is...' She paused, 'she's scared! Let me tell you about having a conversation. There is no perfect moment to say what you want. You say what you know about the subject, and you speak the truth.' She laughed. 'Although I often have problems speaking the truth. My point of view is just as important as what they have to say. I don't want anybody doing better than me. Besides, why do I want other people deciding for me, like my sister's friends do for her? No way!'

Iruni changed the subject. She wasn't used to talking about other people's problems for long. She had her own self-interests to consider.

'My mum works as a cook for the temple priest. He is having a party this weekend and she needs help.' She looked at both girls. 'Do you want to help?'

Ainhoa smiled, but Nora was not so sure.

'He doesn't even pay her well,' Iruni explained. 'She has to pay for her bus fare, and she works hard for her money. But she doesn't have a choice. That's why I didn't drop out of school. I don't want to have no skill or no degree. My mother doesn't earn a lot, and I don't want to do the same.'

Ainhoa nodded. 'I'll go. It sounds exciting.'

They both looked at Nora.

She looked first at Ainhoa and then Iruni before speaking. And when she did, it was with hesitation. 'I don't know. I have to go. See you later.'

Iruni looked at Ainhoa. 'I'll call you later.' Then she turned to Nora. 'Hey, wait up. I want to talk to you.'

Nora stopped to wait.

'You look so lost.'

Nora exhaled. 'My father was by my side my whole life. He encouraged me to try new things, like painting and languages. My mum and dad and I were always busy, doing something. Now, my mum works and I feel so lost like...' She stopped and looked away.

Iruni's eyes widened with a look of innocence. 'Like

me? Like my friends, the lost ones? I know what they call us, and I don't care what they say. Eneko has two parents who work full time and he's on his own. Aitor is an only child, and his parents spoil him too much.'

Nora had never seen her friend look so vulnerable before. 'And you?'

'My mum works long hours for little money. My father left so long ago; I can't even remember his face. I need attention. Most parents keep their children busy like yours. These lost ones give me what I need, what I don't have at home. I need your help with the temple priest.'

Nora nodded. 'Ok, yeah, I guess. I'll go too.' *It was an opportunity to do something different.*

'Good! Let's take the bus there on Saturday.'

'Should we tell Olatz?'

'Oh no. Olatz is cool, but she is in love with herself. She's always looking in the mirror and putting on tight clothes to show off her body. She needs to stop obsessing over herself so much.'

The temple priest's mansion was impressive: a two-storey red brick building with over twenty rooms. A wall surrounded a spacious garden, and an iron gate marked the entrance to the front. When the prior priest De la Torre occupied it, he led a more modest lifestyle, but now since Icono, the new temple priest, took over, he hosted social events every weekend.

The party was just starting when the girls arrived. As

they opened the front gate, a dog barked angrily at the intrusion.

'The temple priest has a big vicious dog that roams around at night,' Iruni said, noticing her friends flinching at the sound. 'I am glad it's locked up in the back.'

Once inside, Ainhoa went to help Iruni's mother while the two girls walked into the large room to get more dinnerware. Icono had decorated the mansion like a museum, with oil paintings, statues and antiques throughout the house.

'Hey, look at that necklace,' Iruni said, licking her lips and imagining it hanging around her neck.

Nora stepped closer to look at it. 'Wow, it looks expensive. It looks like something Cleopatra would wear!'*

The necklace was sitting in an enclosed display case and was draped around a black velvet display stand to show off its magnificence. It was large and formed in a collar shape made of platinum with gold trim. There were three precious gemstones in the centre.

'I want it!' said Iruni without embarrassment. 'He won't know who took it with all these guests.'

Nora stepped back. 'You can't take it!'

'Why? Do you want it?'

'No. It's stealing. It's not right.'

Just then they stopped when a slight sound came down the dim-lit hallway. Nora took a step forward and peered into the gloom, but no other sound arose.

---

* Discover more about Cleopatra's polyglot abilities. She was the last Pharaoh of the Ptolemaic dynasty that started after the death of Alexander the Great.

'I'll take it!' snapped Iruni as she reached out for the necklace.

Just then, the priest's servant walked in. He was a tall mundane man with a sour look on his face, wearing a jacket with sleeves too short for his long arms.

'What are you two up to?' He spoke in a condescending manner, looking down at them as if they were his own servants. 'Come on! Your friend broke some dishes.'

'We'll come back for it later,' She whispered to Nora.

A few hours later, after their chores were done, the two girls returned to the room only to find the necklace was gone. Iruni hissed like an annoyed snake as she searched around. Suddenly, she shouted in triumph. 'Look! There it is.'

Nora followed Iruni's pointing finger. 'Where?'

'It's down the hall!'

'Who moved it down there?'

'Who cares! It's still here and I want it. Let's get it!'

The necklace was at the end of the dim-lit hallway, sitting on a table next to a door. In the distance the two girls could hear the sounds of music and laughter coming from the party. With their eyes transfixed on the spectacular necklace, Iruni pushed Nora to move forward quickly before anyone came this way.

Nora stopped and whispered, 'Something is wrong. There is a shadow moving near the door. Let's turn back.'

When Iruni didn't reply, she turned around and saw her still standing at the entrance of the hall. She hadn't moved. Nora rushed out of the hallway.

'Hey, you let me go in by myself!'

Iruni replied with a fearful look. 'No, no. I stopped because I wanted to get my phone light out of my pocket.'

She changed the subject. 'Let's wait. I can get it later.' She had seen something too.

'Where are my fossils!' Nora said, raising her voice to her friends the day after the party. Nora never raised her voice like this. 'I want them back!'

'They're at the priest's house. They were in my bag, and I left it there by accident,' answered Ainhoa. 'Besides, you never asked for them back. I wasn't sure that you wanted them.'

'We always leave our fossils with each other. I want them back now! They belonged to my father.'

Nora had noticed that Ainhoa's personality had changed recently, and she acted more like Iruni, who never admitted being at fault.

Iruni interjected. 'Well, ok, ok. Let's get them back. I don't know what the temple priest will say. You may have to buy them back.' She paused. 'Do you have money?'

It was cloudy and rainy the day they went back to the priest's office at the church. He greeted them. 'Hey, you three are back to sell or buy? I have plenty of things for sale.'

'We came for the fossils and school bag we forgot during the party at the country house,' said Iruni.

'What?' He frowned and hesitated before he spoke. 'I

am afraid they are not for sale. I like the collection and they look rare as well. They could be precious. Besides, who is going to pay for my dinner plates you broke yesterday?' he said unashamedly. 'Look, I'll tell you what I'll do for you. I'll sell them back to you for one hundred euros.'

'One hundred euros!' Nora exclaimed. 'You only gave us thirty euros for Ainhoa's fossils.'

'That was the price I was willing to pay. You could have walked away. Everything for a price. Think about it. I don't have them here anyway, but I'll get them when you have the money.'

They walked out of the office with sullen faces.

'I know what to do,' Iruni said. 'I didn't see them in his office. We'll go to his house and get them.'

Nora stopped walking. 'Steal them?'

'I said get them back. Do you want them or not?'

'It wouldn't be prudent.'

'Prudent? Ha!' replied Iruni. 'Do you always play it safe and never take chances? You sound like my grandpa. Prudent! Bah!' she repeated. 'Do you know what he talks about now? He talks about how he should have taken more chances. The places he never visited. The girls he was too shy to talk to. That's all he talks about! Do you want your fossils back or not? Besides, I want to get that necklace. I'll help you if you help me. My mum says that the servant goes out to do errands in the evening and Icono usually stays at the church for mass the following morning. It's a perfect time to go to the mansion.'

'How do we distract the dog?' Ainhoa asked, biting her lip.

'I know,' answered Iruni. 'Let's go to the front gate

with food and let the dog out. Then, we will climb the wall. Who will go with me?'

'I'll go,' Ainhoa said, fidgeting with her fingers.

Nora nodded in agreement too.

Iruni grinned. 'I think you should look out and give the dog food. Nora should come in with me and help me find the fossils and the necklace. Come on, let's do it!'

The three girls returned to the country house later that night. It had rained earlier, and their footsteps broke the quiet of the night as they walked through the puddles. In the distance, they could hear the dog barking, reminding them of the danger. The three girls approached the gate.

'The dog must be in another part of the garden,' said Iruni. 'Great! Open the gate, put the food down and stay back and hide,' she commanded Ainhoa. 'We will go in when the dog comes out. OK?'

The two girls, with white faces, shook their heads in agreement.

Ainhoa had brought cooked meat from home, and she put the pieces every few feet outside the grounds. She rattled the gate then ran down the road. The dog either heard the gate or smelled the meat. Regardless of the reason, it came running towards the front of the house. The dog stopped and hesitated. It was not accustomed to going past the gate. It walked outside and started following the trail of meat, gobbling it up along the way as if it had not eaten for hours. When it was far enough away, Nora and Iruni climbed the wall and crossed the grounds as fast as they could.

The house was in darkness all but for a few lights that shone from the windows. Where the light spilled into the garden, it illuminated some bushes and a cypress tree growing just outside the main door. They felt exposed and vulnerable out in the open so crept towards a door at the side of the house. Nora's heart pounded in her chest, and she felt sure someone would hear it.

'If the door is locked, we can try the windows,' whispered Iruni. 'There is always an open window.'

They pushed at the door, and it opened with a creak. They entered the building and started walking through the rooms. The few lowlights flickered shadows on the wall, like ghosts floating, and they started walking through the rooms. They halted when a slight noise came from upstairs.

'It may be the temple priest,' Nora said in a low voice.

As they approached the room where they had seen the necklace, they saw marble statues, old paintings, large flower pots and antiques from around the world. On the opposite side of the large room, a door stood open. Inside, they found the necklace in a display case standing near the door they had just entered. Not too far from the necklace case, on a table lay Ainhoa's bag and Nora's fossil collection. Just then, footsteps echoed towards the door on the opposite side of the room. They froze not knowing what to do. What if they got caught? They needed to hide. But where? They squeezed behind an enormous statue and stood frozen, unable to move as a gigantic shadow approached with a light. It was Icono! Something didn't look quite right. The priest looked frightened.

In his hand, he held a long-stemmed church candle. It flickered as he approached and cast large shadows that danced on the floor. As he crossed the room, he looked from side to side, as if he was looking for someone. When he saw the girls hiding behind the statue he yelled out, before recognising them. Then relief spread across his face, and he quickly composed himself.

'What are you two doing here?' asked Icono, frowning and red faced. 'Come, come, what's going on?'

Iruni held her head high. 'We came for Nora's fossil collection that you stole from her.'

Icono pulled a handkerchief from his pocket and wiped away the sweat that was running down his forehead. 'I'll call the police right now.'

Nora interrupted and said, 'We heard a noise upstairs and thought it was you.'

'De la Torre is out of his room.' He patted his brow once more as panic rose again in him.

The girls weren't used to seeing him this way - vulnerable and frightened rather than arrogant and condescending.

'De la Torre?' replied the two girls at once.

'The prior priest?' Nora asked with a surprised look.

'Yes, the prior priest. He is still here but has dementia. His condition has worsened, and he has become aggressive. He's two metres tall and weighs twenty stone and is as strong as a bull. I need help!' Desperation showed in his face. 'The servant is out on errands. I don't think I can take De la Torre back to his room by myself. I have to give him his medicine to sedate him and make him sleep.'

'Call the police,' said Iruni.

The priest gasped. 'No, oh dear no. It would look bad for the church. If the police looked at this collection...' he paused, 'they might ask questions.'

'Everything for a price,' came Iruni's sarcastic reply.

He continued. 'I need your help. With the three of us, we can get him back to his room and lock the door. I'll give you back your fossils. Now, follow me.'

He turned around and started walking to the other room. Iruni walked up behind the priest as he was walking past the door, and she slammed the door shut.

'What are you doing?' a surprised Nora asked.

'I don't want to help him!'

'You said you would!'

'I said that to shut him up. Did you think we were going to help him stop a madman?'

Icono started banging on the door that the girls had just locked, but he stopped when the dog started barking right outside the window of the room that the two girls were in.

'Did you close the gate when we ran in?' asked Iruni.

'No, I was too busy running after you.'

'The dog must have come back and is outside the window. He's suspicious. He must have smelled our scent.'

'We're trapped.' Nora could feel the tears pricking at her eyes and her heart beat harder. 'Call the police!'

'No, no, how do we explain ourselves here?'

Nora pointed to the windows opposite each other in the room. 'Let's distract the dog from this window and open the opposite window where Ainhoa is waiting and climb the wall to get out. You distract the dog and let me know when the coast is clear, and we'll go for the wall.'

'Wait!' commanded Iruni. 'Grab the necklace first.'

Nora started walking towards the necklace but

stopped. She turned to face Iruni. 'If you want the necklace, you get it.'

'And your fossil collection?'

'I don't want it. I don't want to steal. It's only material things. I can buy another collection.'

Iruni, unaccustomed to following commands, went to take the necklace.

'The door!' cried Nora. 'First check if the other door is locked in case someone comes back.'

Despite the nasty look, Iruni said nothing. She walked up to the door and locked it before turning her attention to the necklace. As she was about to take it, her phone interrupted the silence. She pulled it out and read the message. 'Ainhoa wrote that the servant is coming in the front gate. Let's get out!'

Nora pointed towards the door that Iruni had just locked. 'Look!'

The doorknob was moving. They both looked at each other wide eyed.

Iruni cried out. 'It must be De la Torre.'

They opened the window opposite of where the dog was barking. Nora and Iruni jumped down and started running towards the stone wall. Ainhoa was waiting for them, standing on something behind the wall. Her eyes and mouth opened wide in shock, and she screamed. 'Run!'

They both started running faster. The dog had come around the corner. They heard its barking getting louder as it came closer. With terror in their hearts, they ran faster, towards the wall. Some logs lay at the foot of the wall that they jumped onto and used to climb up, ignoring the scrapes to the skin on their hands and legs.

They reached the top of the wall just as the dog caught up with them. Swinging their legs over they dropped to the other side, leaving the dog still jumping against the bricks and barking as he tried to catch their legs.

Nora had a little over one month to write a fifteen-page report. She remembered the method that her teachers had suggested. First, brainstorming, then writing general ideas around the topic and assigning each idea to the body of the essay. She knew it was important to think about the beginning, the middle and the end. Second, to make an outline of these ideas and write a few sentences in each paragraph. Then, she wanted to work on the essay a few hours a day, take a break and come back to revise and write more. Finally, she knew she wanted to finish it a few days before the deadline to let her mother read it for suggestions and corrections. During one of her breaks from writing, she went to talk to her mother.

'Mum, I found some things in Papi's old wooden chest. This watch and compass look old. The watch has the initials of CM with a note saying Carlos Morgan? Who's that?'

Her mother shrugged. 'I don't know.'

'Also,' Nora was hesitant to ask the question, 'who is Valentina? There were letters and other papers with her name mentioned.'

Her mother stopped what she was doing and looked at Nora. 'She was his ex-wife.'

'What?'

Her mother and father were not married and that was

fine for her. She had never asked them why not. It was common for her friends' parents to be unmarried, a single parent, or a stepparent.

'Yes, he was married. I'm not sure why he never told you. When the marriage didn't work out, he emigrated to Europe,' her mother said as she cleaned her hands on a towel.

Nora, still processing the information, asked, 'Who is Carlos Morgan? A half-brother? An uncle? Someone close to his ex-wife?'

'I don't know.' She looked serious but not angry, just genuinely curious about who Carlos Morgan might be. 'He always wanted to live in Europe. He got a job teaching in Spain, and that's when we met. Your father taught English, but he didn't like it.'

Nora raised her eyebrows. 'He didn't like it?'

'Do people who speak Spanish want to become English teachers?' her mother asked, raising her eyebrows.

'Well, no.'

'Well, he didn't either. He came here with little money. He needed a job. Because of his age and heavy Spanish accent, he couldn't find another job other than teaching English.'

'Papi spoke Spanish with an accent?'

A faint smile came to her mother's face. 'Spanish wasn't his native language, but you grew up with him and didn't notice the way he spoke.'

'Learning English in Spain is popular. There are many English academies. Like the one you studied at for years. The schools are private, and the students directly pay the owner of the academy. All the pressure is on the teacher's shoulders. The owner of the academy is always asking the students if they like the teacher. The owner often sits outside the door to listen to what the teacher is saying. He left after a few years, but the academies always asked him to come back. He prepared a lot to understand a new grammar textbook every course.'

Her mother sat down. 'Most native English teachers come from the United Kingdom or Ireland. They are usually young and want to live abroad for a short time, so they find a teaching job to pay rent. Then, they return home. There is a big turnover of English teachers. He knew if he stayed, he wouldn't find a job he liked.'

'Did he want to return to his country?'

'Yes, especially when he got anxious about his job prospects. He worked as a teacher to support us.'

'Why did he stay if he didn't enjoy teaching?'

'He stayed for us. He loved you,' her mother replied proudly.

'Does he have more children? Do I have brothers or sisters?'

'I don't know. I don't think so, but he never mentioned his ex-wife or prior life much. Although he told me once that she was from South America, and she returned home. Do you want to find her by searching the Internet?'

'I don't know, maybe,' shrugged Nora. She realised she had a very childlike idea of her father. She didn't know him at all. *Who was he? What kind of life did he have when he was younger? Do I have family there?*

'Your father took you to the U.S. when you were around four years old, but we never went back,' her mother explained. 'You have many cousins who are older.

They were in their twenties when you visited them for the first time. After that trip, he often took you to Ireland and the United Kingdom.'

~

Later that day, Nora went to the Plaza Moraza to meet with her friends. The boys from the lost ones were sitting apart watching their dogs play-fight. As she walked up to the group of girls, Iruni was bragging about what had happened at the temple priest's mansion. 'We should go back and do it again,' she said with bravado.

Ainhoa was smiling too.

'I am not going back,' Nora said. "I don't want to steal anything.' She crossed her arms and pouted to show her defiance.

'Come on! What good is it to be nice all the time?' Iruni flicked her head towards Nora, a sign of disrespect.

'Why are you always trying to make us do things we don't want to do? What good is it to have so much free time? What have you done since you dropped out of English class? Not much. I have learned English. I also learned how to draw. Something that I love. So what, you smoke and have a small tattoo. What does that mean? You had a few boyfriends that you said were not good to you? I kept busy after school with classes or hanging out with my mum.'

The boys, sitting next to their dogs, stopped and watched what would happen next. Iruni, Ainhoa and a few other girls looked at Nora in silence. They had never seen her speak out like this. Nora turned and started walking away. Iruni whispered something to the others.

They laughed. Nora didn't look back and kept on walking.

Ainhoa got up and ran towards Nora and said, 'Wait! I want to talk to you.'

Nora turned around to look at her friend. 'Come on! Come home with me and we can have fun like we used to. Eating chocolate and looking at our bug and fossil collections, imagining that we are treasure hunters.'

Ainhoa hesitated for a moment as she looked at Nora and said, 'I don't want to look at fossils or bugs anymore. I want to hang out with my new friends. Come with me!' she pleaded. 'Come back and hang out with us. Besides, Olatz is coming soon.'

Nora shook her head and turned away.

Ainhoa said in desperation, 'I'll give you the rest of my fossil collection later. I don't want it anymore.'

Nora didn't respond but simply turned and walked home, alone.

Towards the end of the school year, Nora was finishing her fifteen-page paper. She took a break from writing to talk to her mother.

'I have contacted a few people in Argentina through social media over the last few weeks,' Nora said in a serious tone to her mother. 'A woman from Buenos Aires responded and said she knew Papi. She doesn't want to explain about her family by email to someone she doesn't know. I'd like to visit her.'

'It's a long way,' her mother said with a worried

expression. 'I don't think you should go alone. It's so far and you are too young.'

Her mother could tell that her daughter was determined to go.

'I never told you what the bullies were saying to me. They made fun of Papi, saying that he was an old grandpa and a tourist who never left. Besides, I want to know his history and to see if I have family in South America. I also have a friend in Peru. I'd like to visit her and go to Machu Picchu, too, like Papi wanted.'

'How will you pay for it?'

'I don't know how.'

'I might know a way,' her mother said with a smile. 'You are a beneficiary on your father's bank account.'

'I thought Papi had little money.'

'He didn't. We paid the rent with my full-time job. He had little savings and lived on social security. On his own, he would have lived on the streets with only his social security payments. Something that I don't understand,' she paused, 'is that he invested in stocks.'

Her interest peaked. 'Stocks? What's that?'

'Yeah, stocks,' her mother answered. 'Companies that need to raise money to invest and sustain their product offer stock to the public to raise cash. He bought stocks from the most well-known companies, like international tech and pharmaceutical companies. He let the stocks grow for over thirty years. I, too, have savings for you,' her mother smiled, 'but in a savings account. You have a few thousand euros in the bank. The interest on a savings account is less than one percent, which is pathetic. The savings account earns about ten euros a year. Your father often said there is a better chance of finding ten euros at the park than earning euros from a savings account.' Her mother took a paper and pen from a drawer. 'You have inherited about 80,000 euros. It is for your education if you decide to study abroad. Stocks are not guaranteed,' her mother explained to Nora. 'If the business does well, your stock goes up and makes more money, but if the business does not do well, you lose your money. I told him not to do it because I don't know anything about it. I think you can just sell the stock and take the money, but I won't allow you to take all the money out at once. It's for your education.'

Nora returned to her bedroom, trying to make sense of it all. She knew she had to concentrate on her essay and keep all the adventurous dreams from clouding her writing.

Towards the last month of school, 'You passed the written exam!' Eskarne said with a big smile to Nora. 'All of your teachers were excited. We only have a few more weeks of school and you are going to university!'

Nora smiled for an instance and said, 'I don't think that I am going to study abroad next year. I plan to take a gap year and reapply at a later date. I want to know who my father was.'

PART III

Nora took the aeroplane from Spain to Miami, in the U.S., then to Buenos Aires. It was a long flight and Nora was happy to eventually get off the plane. She stretched and yawned while collecting her bags, but she didn't feel tired for long. The buzz in the airport from the multitude of people amazed her and gave her more energy. She looked for a cash machine and took the bus to the city to her hotel in the neighbourhood of Recoleta. Nora had written to Valentina, who had given her her address. When Nora arrived at her front door, the woman who answered gave one kiss, as was the custom in Argentina, to her young acquaintance. She was in her 60s and still dignified.

'I met you father here in Buenos Aires,' Valentina said with a strong Argentine accent. 'A year later, we got married at the town hall. It happened so fast. It was very difficult to leave my family and my job, but I left it all because I loved him. After we got married, he returned home first while I was waiting for my green card. I remember all he had as he returned home was his plane ticket, a small suitcase and a few hundred dollars. He was a penniless wanderer, but I loved him. I would have followed him anywhere.'

They sat down in the kitchen. 'While I was living in the U.S., I didn't know English and I was so far from my family. It was the first time I had ever left my country. We always struggled with money and that caused stress at home. I remember we used to go to libraries to read books, drink coffee and have a snack there. While most people went to bars, we would hang out at the library.' She laughed while thinking about the time. 'We moved a lot, because he changed jobs many times, never happy with any of them. To make the situation worse, we couldn't get pregnant. After seven years of trying to get pregnant, it took its toll. After eight years, I had had enough.'

Nora listened, trying not to interrupt but sipping the drink Valentina had offered her.

'My mum had cancer,' Valentina explained. 'I wanted to go home. He wanted to emigrate to Europe. We had little money. We would have to start from zero in Europe. It was his dream, not mine,' she said with remorse.

'Why did he want to emigrate to Europe?'

She thought before she spoke. 'Your father was disappointed in his country.' He said there was a rise of division between race, class and gender. The television programmes added fuel to the fire when they acted like the news hour but were political commentators using fear and propaganda to divide the country. The internal division with external competition from other countries would weaken the United States. Many people, including his friends and neighbours, believed in lies based on fear.'

She got up to put on the kettle. 'I returned home and had to start from nothing. It was horrible. It took me two years to find a job. My father, brother and sister helped me while I looked for work. I never wanted to experience that pain again.'

'Do you have children?'

'No,' she said grimly. 'I have nephews and nieces. Ironically, when I came back from the U.S., I found out that I was pregnant.'

'You were pregnant with his child?'

'Yes, but I lost the baby. I woke up one night bleeding. I screamed for my parents to help me. We didn't know what was happening. They took me to the hospital and the doctor told me I had lost the baby.'

Nora wanted to find out something that she had waited a long time to ask. 'Who is Carlos Morgan?'

The elderly woman smiled. 'His name was Charles Morgan, and he was my great grandfather from England on my mother's side. He was a civil engineer, and he came to build the railroads. He was working in Buenos Aires when he met my great grandmother.'

'I found a compass and watch with his initials and a note with his name on it in my father's trunk.'

'The compass and watch belonged to Charles, and I gave them to your father. I knew how much he liked antiques. Let me explain something to you,' Valentina said in a calm voice. 'There were many European immigrants coming here. Loads of Italians, Spanish,

German and some English arrived as well. My great-grandfather Charles was one of them.'

'Immigrants from Europe came to the Americas, including Canada, the U.S.A. and South America. Argentina was the leading producer of agriculture in the world, and the pampas grasslands were rich in agriculture. My country experienced huge economic growth. It grew by six percent per year. There was an abundance of land and a need for labour. Europeans had few employment opportunities back home and many religious restrictions in their countries. One out of four people who lived in Argentina at the time were immigrants, according to books I have read. Many Spanish came from the region of Galicia. That is why we call Spanish *Gallegos*,' she said with no malice.

'The English immigrants influenced Argentine culture. That's why we have sports like rugby, polo, football and field hockey. My great-grandfather was one of these English immigrants. It's a shame we can't revitalise our country like before. We have so many natural resources.'

Valentina took the empanadas out of the oven while she continued. 'Starting around 1950, Argentina suffered a decline because of political and economic instability. We had dictators who attacked academics and professors.'

'Why attack teachers and professors? They seem the most harmless,' Nora asked.

'Because the dictators feared them. Professors were educated and didn't believe the propaganda or lies that the political leaders were saying. Look around the world. Any country that has an autocratic leader who wants to stay in power usually restricts the press and jails academics who could threaten their reign.'

'Slowly, our situation improved until the year 2001. The peso was about the same value as the U.S. dollar and the banks allowed us to withdraw either pesos or dollars. That's when the economic crisis began; high inflation caused the peso to drop suddenly and rapidly. The people panicked and went to the bank to withdraw their money in dollars. It was a more stable currency.'

'All the banks closed and opened days later. They only allowed pesos to be taken out with a lot less value. People lost their life savings. There is a distrust of banks and politicians. This loss of wealth leads to other consequences as well.'

'Too much serious talk,' she said to her young friend. 'You are here only for a week? That's a long way to come for a brief stay. Take advantage of your time here. I'll show you around Buenos Aires and the places that your father liked.'

They explored Buenos Aires with its wide, chaotic boulevards and stopped in the neighbourhood called La Boca. There were local artists selling artwork on the street.

They stopped at one of the painter's booths and Nora pointed at a painting. 'I have seen this neighbourhood from a picture that we have at the house in Bilbao.'

'La Boca was traditionally the place where immigrants arrived in Buenos Aires,' Valentia explained. 'They were usually poor, so they painted their houses to cover up the dilapidated materials they used to build them.'

'I also have seen this painting from a school textbook,' Nora said, while trying to remember the details of the painting. 'What is it about?'

'It's a painting of the Basque explorer Juan de Garay discovering Buenos Aires.'

'There is a road called Juan de Garay where I live in Bilbao. Who was he?'

'He was one of the Spanish explorers who founded Buenos Aires and other important cities in South America.'

Nora took out the compass and watch that she had brought from home. 'You gave this to my father because he loved antiques, but I think it is better to return this to your family.'

Valentina smiled as she took the objects and gave her young friend a hug.

Lima, Peru. As Nora arrived in Lima, her friend Elsi met her at the airport with a hug. 'You can stay with me at my house before going to Cusco. As I told you before you arrived, my father works long hours at his sewing shop, and I help him. My mother is an English teacher and teaches at a public school. They saved a lot to improve my life and sent me to study abroad. That's why I was hesitant to sneak out to the museum in Cambrian. It was an enormous sacrifice by my parents to send me there. I was lucky too. I got a financial aid scholarship to study.'

As they arrived at Elsi's house, she explained her plan to study abroad while showing Nora her guest bedroom.

'I do not know if I want to go to America or Europe for a better life. I don't want to leave my family and friends. My parents say it's for the best. I went abroad already to the U.S. and Wales for the summer. I went to see if I could adjust. I'd like to go to university abroad. I'll look for work while I study to help pay for school. My parents have saved three years' worth of tuition fees for me to study. That leaves the fourth year to pay. My mum tells me if I emigrate, I have to be strong. If I get accepted and pay for my university fees, I will have as much right as anyone, although some people don't think so. I noticed animosity between certain countries. Some Europeans have a problem with the current world powers like the U.S. and their foreign policies. Have you forgotten your own past?'

Nora shook her head. 'Yeah, but that was history. We don't blame ourselves for what happened. We don't talk about it. Especially us, I mean teenagers. We often talk about ourselves, our friends or classmates.'

'That's hypocritical, don't you think? Europeans having problems with the current world power and not remembering your history.'

Nora had seen this before, people expressing honest facts, but others would never admit the truth and argue to the contrary using opinions to justify their beliefs. She shrugged. 'I don't know what to say.'

Elsi motioned to Nora to follow her back to the kitchen. 'My mum says there are no angels or saints in this world. There is no innocent country. You speak

Spanish and see how challenging it is to be in another country. Imagine if you couldn't speak the language?'

Nora changed the subject. 'Why not go back to Wales? You loved it.'

'Because they stopped giving out scholarships.'

'Why? What happened?'

Elsi looked at her firmly. 'Have you talked with anyone from the summer class in Wales?'

'No. I haven't. I hung out with you and Gwen and...' she paused, 'Owain. I've lost touch with Gwen.'

'Do you know what happened after the theft?'

Nora spoke in an unconvincing manner. 'Well, they removed Seren, the art teacher, from her teaching position pending an investigation and Gwynfor was going to be reinstated as director.'

'That didn't happen. Gwynfor briefly returned to his position as director and refused to press charges against Seren. He lost his job for overspending. She also left her position due to stress from her arrest.' Elsi asked in a low voice, 'Did you hear the rumour?'

'What rumour?'

'That night you received that note about meeting Owain at the museum. He got one too. Well, they say there was a third note.'

'A third note?'

'Yes,' Elsi said, the pitch of her voice rising.

'Who got it?'

'Seren. Rumour has it that she received it the same night telling her about the missing artwork.'

Nora's mouth dropped open.

Elsi continued, 'She didn't take the tunnel to the museum or leave by it to get to church. Seren didn't know they were open. The school had sealed them off years ago. She wasn't aware of their use.'

'Llewellyn is now the director. He cut almost all the scholarships. It was Llewellyn who had taken away Owain's mobile phone earlier that day.'

Nora listened to everything that Elsi had just said. Could she be guilty of having two people lose their jobs?

Elsi had to go to work. She was going to the door when she stopped and said, 'He asks about you a lot?'

'Who?'

'Owain. We still talk through messaging. Maybe you should write to him. I think he would like it.'

Nora stood there like a statue, perplexed, as her friend left for work. While Elsi worked, Nora explored Lima. She took her notebook to draw sketches of famous buildings and write notes in the Miraflores neighbourhood.

Elsi returned home after work and said, 'Let's talk about the trip to Machu Picchu. There are two popular ways to get there: taking the train or hiking. Taking a train is nice and it takes about three hours, but I would recommend walking up the Inca Trail. It takes about three or four days, but the experience is unforgettable. I think it's best to hire guides to take you to Machu Picchu. I don't think you should go by yourself. Leave your suitcase here and only take your backpack with rain gear and a warm sweater. I'll go with you if you can wait until I finish helping my father.'

'I'll go to Cusco to look for a guide and explore for a few days.'

'You can always stay here and wait, even though you are probably bored,' answered Elsi. 'You shouldn't go by yourself. If you go with a tourist group, you can go to Cusco with a travel agency.'

A day later, at a travel agency, they found a group of about twenty people wanting to visit Machu Picchu. The group had a mixture of Europeans, North Americans and Asians. Nora joined them.

As Nora was departing, Elsi reminded her, 'Stay with the group. Don't go alone anywhere. Call me if you have any problems. I'll arrive in three days. Be careful.'

Cusco, Peru is the starting point to Machu Picchu. Spanish colony buildings were evident, especially in the town centre. Crowded narrow streets with marketplaces full of people were everywhere. Stray dogs were running around looking for their next meal among the sellers' stalls. World travellers, speaking in many foreign languages, explored the city. The local economy depends on tourism, and every traveller was welcomed. On the sides of hills, as far as the eye can see, there were houses built in the traditional style. From out of them came native inhabitants walking the long hills to arrive at the city centre to sell their wares.

Nora arrived by plane to Cusco with a tourist group. A tall, heavy-set man, American judging by his accent, was escorting a group of tourists already. He was wearing an official tour guide badge around his neck.

He stopped by Nora and said with a smile, 'Hi, I'm Tony. You must be going to Machu Picchu? I am an official guide. We have a small bus to give tourists a ride to the hotel.'

He spoke to the bus driver in a mixture of Quechua and Spanish. 'It's eighty-five soles. Pay the man for the bus ride,' he said to Nora.

Her face turned red as she said, 'Oh, sorry,' and paid the bus driver.

The tourist group arrived at the hotel. Tony walked up to her and said, 'The train trip is four hundred dollars. You can stay in your own room, or there is an elderly Canadian woman who has a large room with beds to spare. It's two-hundred-and-sixty euros for the three nights at the hotel.'

'Two-hundred-and-sixty euros? That much?' she said with a confused expression. She had euros, so she knew it was more valuable than the Peruvian soles, the local currency. The hotel seemed expensive. 'The sign at the counter says One-hundred-and-sixty Peruvian soles per night.'

Tony pouted. 'Oh, that sign is outdated. The prices have changed.'

'It's too much,' Nora repeated.

He grinned and took his hat off to scratch his hair. 'It's common here to charge higher fees to tourists than the local population,' he said with a hint of anger. 'They prefer dollars to euros. I have dollars. I can do a money exchange for a fee.'

Not knowing what to say, 'I'll pay for the hotel tomorrow, but not the train,' she said. 'I'll have to go to the bank. I'll pay in Peruvian currency, not euros.'

The elderly Canadian approached and Tony said to both of them, 'Come on, let's catch up with the rest of the group. They are going to have a drink at the restaurant. We can talk later.'

Nora didn't have time to think about what had just happened.

At the bar, Nora spoke to the retired Canadian woman. She discovered her name was Beverly and she was a retired teacher. Beverley was a kind and welcoming person, and during the conversation, Nora asked her new friend about the prices to Machu Picchu. She had already paid for the tour, but there were out-of-pocket expenses they had to pay.

Nora walked up to Tony, who was at the bar, as he said, 'We need to pay for the drinks.' He spoke in Quechua and Spanish to the bartender. The bartender said *twelve* soles, but he spoke too fast.

Tony turned to her and said, 'Everybody owes twenty soles for their drink. Please pay the waiter.' He again spoke Quechua and Spanish to the bartender. 'Hold on to the change. I'll be back to pick it up later.'

Nora pulled a face, like she couldn't believe what she was hearing. She had spoken to Tony in English since they first met. She told him she was from the Basque country, and because of her name, maybe he didn't realise that Spanish was her first language.

Later that night, she called Elsi.

'Wow, that seems too expensive for your hotel and trip up the mountain,' Elsi said. 'There are cheaper hotels that are just as nice. I heard of an American who had his business shut down in Cusco due to overcharging visitors. Be careful of him. They said he tries to take advantage of travellers going to Machu Picchu. Have you already paid for the trip?'

'No, only the hotel room until Monday.'

'Good, don't pay. I'll arrive by Tuesday. We will hire a guide to walk up the Inca path.'

Nora winced. 'I know you are working and taking time off.'

'Don't worry! I much prefer to go with you up the Inca Trail.' Her voice betraying her excitement.

Nora went to her room and met Beverly there. 'I am not going with the group by train,' Nora told her roommate. 'Tony is charging too much for everything. I plan to spend the night here and wait for my friend from Lima to go with me.'

The following Tuesday, Elsi arrived and explained about the hike up the mountain.

'The Inca Trail is the original road used between Cuzco and Machu Picchu.'

Nora took out her notebook to write notes. 'Why did the Incas build so high in the mountains?'

'The word Machu Picchu means old mountain or old peak. It's not a large place. It has about two hundred buildings and is surrounded by agricultural terraces. Scholars think it was a religious place or resort for the Inca emperor and elites. The Incas believed the sun was an important aspect of their religion. There are stones there that were astronomically aligned with the sun.'

Elsi paused to let Nora write and then explained the history. 'Hiram Bingham, a professor of history at Yale, studied South American history and dreamed of what secrets and lost cities were there. He was the first scholar to discover Machu Picchu. It was remote, and because of time and nature, it stayed hidden for centuries, only known by Peruvian farmers.'

The first day, waking up before dawn, Nora and her small group started the upward climb. She and Elsi followed their porters, who were friendly, wiry and carried heavy backpacks. They provided guidance and help to set up camp for the girls. The trail pitched upwards with many up and down slopes, only accessible by foot. As the mist and fog cleared, the views from the mountain were revealed. For the next few hours, the girls climbed the twisting slopes going up and down as they made their staggered ascent up stairs carved into the mountainside to help them climb upwards.

Nora marvelled at the concept of making these steps without modern tools. In the late afternoon, the two girls, both worn out, were relieved to arrive at camp. They were told that day two was the worst.

The second day consisted of walking from ten thousand feet to thirteen thousand feet. At such a high altitude, the heart has to work a lot harder because of less oxygen. They woke up before sunrise. The trail, like the first day, undulated up and down and they climbed up thousands of stairs for hours. Rain started falling, making the path slippery, but the two never complained as they hiked in wet clothes. It was a slow and steady pace. After stopping for lunch, they carried on walking for a few more hours before stopping to camp. Luckily, the campsite was well equipped with hot running water and flushing toilets.

The third day they woke up to a heavy mist, but the sun quickly burned it away and they had clear views of the Andes mountains and snow-capped peaks. Day four was the day they arrived. The trail approached Machu Picchu from above so that they were looking down on it. From this vantage point, it was even more impressive. They had to pass a checkpoint, where their documents were examined, then they were free to explore the city. The construction of these ruins was astounding. There was a large sun stone that was astronomically aligned with the sun and summer solstice.

Nora thought about her parents and whispered, 'I wish they were with me to share this wonderful experience.'

After spending hours exploring, Elsi said, 'Come on! Let's give gifts to the guides.'

They took a bus to Aguas Calientes to begin their descent back to Cusco.*

Eighteen-year-old Nora was getting dressed in her bedroom in the morning. She had recently come back from her trip to South America. After looking in the mirror, she noticed that her body had changed. Embarrassed by her new shape, she put on a heavier sweater and longer t-shirt underneath and slung her backpack down low on her back.

She had to run some errands. As she was walking to

---

* Agua Calientes is the town below Machu Picchu.

the square that had the trolley train that goes up to Artxanda she ran into her friend Olatz.*

'Hey, Olatz! What's up?' .

'Hey, Nora.' Her friend greeted her with a hug. 'I am going to work at a cafeteria. 'I stopped hanging out with Ainhoa and her friends. They do nothing besides hang out in the plaza and talk about their dogs and motorcycles. She calls me up once a week, crying about Aitor. Anyway, I have to go. See you!'

Nora smiled and waved goodbye. 'Take care.'

She returned home to talk with her mother. 'Everything seems related.'

Her mother dried her hands on the washcloth. 'What do you mean?'

'Wherever I go, there are common themes I have seen travelling. Everyone has different stories but wants the same thing at the end of the day - a fulfilling life. I also realise how unique our planet is, from all the different countries to our solar system.'

Her mother hugged her. 'I've seen you mature and become more self-assured. Your father would be proud. He'd often say that when people stay in one place, they create a bubble of what life is about. Once you travel, you break this bubble and see the world from a different perspective. What are you going to do?'

Nora kissed her mother. 'I am going to apply for university abroad, but first I want to visit someone in Wales.'

---

* Trolley train that goes to Artxanda, a popular tourist attraction above Bilbao.

Nora arrived in Wales and planned to stay for a week. She had done a lot of research to find people by social media. She walked to the public library, to the art room. She saw the person that she was looking for. She approached with an uneasy feeling in her stomach. The person was busy putting away paint supplies.

'Seren?'

The woman with long curly hair turned around. A surprised look came to her face when she saw the person who said her name.

'Oh, Nora, right?'

'Yes, it's me. I wanted to talk to you. I've heard what happened at Cambrian School and I wanted to apologise for my carelessness and the pain that I may have caused.'

A faint smile came to Seren's face. 'It's ok. It was a stressful time for me. It was time for a change. I teach part-time at this library, but I plan to emigrate to Toronto, Canada. I have family there. What are you doing here?'

'I came to visit a friend, but I stopped by here to apologise to you first. All the best to you, Seren.'

'Likewise,' her former art teacher said with a smile.

Nora arrived at Owain's house and met his parents. The following day, they all went camping.

'I told my parents about you. It delighted my parents that I made friends at summer school. You have travelled so much this year. I told them about your South America trip. We have decided to take you to Eryri National Park to hike Yr Wyddfa Mountain and camp for three days.'

'Yeah, I am fortunate to see many wonderful places. I have a world map on my bedroom wall where I mark the places that I have been.'

Owain held his telescope. 'We finished setting up camp and my parents are relaxing. I brought my telescope. Let's look at the planets and stars. Everybody thinks the stars are random in the sky. They are not. They are in the right place by design. Like dropping a stone in the water, the force of the stone creates waves. The force of gravity creates stars as the universe expands.'

Nora pointed with the telescope. 'What's that orange glow?'

'Have you heard of a red giant?'

'I don't remember.'

Owain explained, 'They say this is the time of the stars. The sun is a star and is made from hydrogen and helium. The stars are billions of years old, but they age and burn out. It's so incredible to think that our planet is in the right location. If it were closer, it would be too hot to survive with burning temperatures and no water. If the Earth was farther away, it would be below freezing. A red giant is a star that is dying. When it depletes all its hydrogen, the core will contract, but the shell of the sun will expand. Its expansion will swallow everything in its path, including its planets - Venus, Mercury and Earth. As the sun cools and becomes a white dwarf, our solar system will remain in darkness forever.'

'Let's worry about keeping the bugs out of sleeping bags first,' Nora said with a smile.

At the end of her week's stay, Owain and his parents gave Nora a ride to the airport.

She could not stop smiling. 'Let's stay in contact and see how it goes.'

He nodded. 'I'm here in Cardiff and you're in Bilbao. I'll visit you when I get a chance.'

She hugged his parents. She smiled at Owain and gave him a hug as well.

AFTERWORD

Discussions for curious people.

1. Why is it important to find your voice and understand that your opinion matters?

2. What are common languages in your area?

3. What languages would you like to learn and why?

4. How can countries preserve their original language?

5. Some countries make learning the original language mandatory, but others have it as optional. Which one do you think is the best method?

6. Are you curious about travelling to other countries? For what reasons?

7. How difficult do you think it is to emigrate to another country?

NOTES

ACKNOWLEDGMENTS

This book, The Evolution of Nora O'Brien Pacheco, has been possible thanks to the collaboration of the following people. I much appreciate Kate (United Kingdom), Lesley (United Kingdom), and Donna (U.S) for all the help and suggestions with editing. I also want to give thanks to the following people for their advice. Patricia (Spain), Grace (U.S), Elisabeth (U.S) and John (U.S).

I algo give thanks to the artist Nabin Karma (India).

Thanks to the BBC article, The Bilbao effect: How 20 years of Gerry's Guggenheim transformed the city.

I left footnotes. Whether or not they help, remains to be seen.

I have also translated the book into Spanish.

ACKNOWLEDGMENTS

ABOUT THE AUTHOR

Kevin O'Flaherty is an indie author who writes about real places using fictional characters. He writes what he considers the most important topic-the interaction between people. This includes the morals, vices, redemption, bravery in the fact of danger, self-esteem and how people treat others. These traits make us unique.

His inspiration in writing literature comes from what he sees, hears and reads in his surroundings.

He arrived in Santander and later to Bilbao with a suitcase and backpack. He's grateful to the Basque and Spanish people, who he considers noble and brave.

He formatted the book using Vellum.

Help support indie authors and ask for this book at your local library.

Https://www.sites.google.com/view/sapereaudelibris

ALSO BY KEVIN O'FLAHERTY

Another book by the author: Short Stories from Faraway Places

A collection of four stories about people at the crossroads of life. The road they take will lead them to positive or negative consequences. It's a story of self-determination and human struggle.

The Garden of the Republic: An impulsive New Yorker who is bored with his life joins an NGO and travels to Tucumán, Argentina to build a health clinic. He meets a few individuals who have a tremendous impact on his stay as he learns about Argentina's Dirty War during the 1980s.

Zabalburu Urkia: An Irishman with slight disabilities sees his life passing by him. He takes a chance and goes to Durango, the Basque Country in Spain, to teach English. Once there, his disabilities make it stressful for him and by accident learns about the lost treasure of the Basque diaspora.

The Bells of Gloucester: Two young lads from Gloucester, England, best friends since childhood, slowly drift apart as their life takes them down different paths. Their new friends make them decide which direction they'll go. It's a story about the pressures of adolescence and redemption.

Celtic Verde: An allegory tale about the only constant in life is change. It uses metaphorical characters who represent the cycles of life-birth, selfishness, hope and death. Connor, a self-centred man from Chicago, with Irish heritage, thinks adolescence will last forever. As an adult, he runs from responsibility. He leaves his elderly parents in their time of need and goes to Ireland to look for work, but discovers how much

Ireland has changed. Desperate, he gets tempted to make a wish at an ancient water well.

Made in the USA
Monee, IL
07 July 2026

56547994R00075